Terse & funny and dry as a dead Iowa
corn snake baking in the sun.
Palecek delivers a quick, deadpan slap to
reactionary, mindless post-9/11 America.
The sting is delightful.

— Mark Morford, *San Francisco Chronicle*,
talking about "Iowa Terror"

"I've read JFK ASSASSINATION FICTION by Don Delillo and Norman Mailer, and can tell you that this new novel (*Johnny Moon*) not only is Mike's best book yet, it's much better than Delillo's and Mailer's efforts to do justice to the most important event in U.S. history.

— Dr. Kevin Barrett

MIKE PALECEK WRITES WITH passion, wit, and always with a strong social conscience.

— Howard Zinn

MIKE PALECEK REMINDS ME of Socrates the gadfly who
asked unwelcome questions, Diogenes with his
lantern looking in vain for an honest man, Chekhov the man with
the hammer challenging the
complacent family to share their meal, Kerouac the ever on the
move, somewhat hysterical searcher, and he reminds me of many
Americans who as children were so blasted with
propaganda that they're
devoting the rest of their lives to challenging the lies and all who tell
them. In this land where babies are brought by storks
and buildings collapse due to
unpatriotic bricks, we need the gadfly because no leader, preacher,
guru, or saint will wake us up, though
the Doomsday Clock is ticking close to twelve.

— David Ray, *American poet*

Cover art by Alison M. Healy

Printed in the U.S.A.
Published by
7th Street Press

SEVENTH
STREET
PRESS

Revolution

by Mike Palecek

"Give me liberty or give me death."

— Patrick Henry

William H. Bonney (born William Henry McCarty, Jr. c. November 23, 1859-c. July 14, 1881), better known as Billy The Kid, was a 19th-century Irish American gunman who participated in the Lincoln County War and became a frontier outlaw of the American Old West. According to legend, he killed 21 men, but it is generally believed that he killed between four and nine. He killed his first man in 1877 at the age of 17, although he could have been as young as 15.

— Wikipedia

"There is something more terrible than a hell of suffering — a hell of boredom."

— Victor Hugo, *Les Misérables*

"And this you can know — fear the time when Manself will not suffer and die for a concept, for this one quality is the foundation of Manself, and this one quality is man, distinctive in the universe."
— *The Grapes of Wrath*

"You know what they want? They want obedient workers. People who are just smart enough to run the machines and do the paper work and just dumb enough to passively accept all these increasingly crappier jobs with the lower pay, the longer hours, the reduced benefits, the end of overtime, and the vanishing pension that disappears the minute you go to collect it.
They own this fucking place.
It's a big club.
And you ain't in it."

— George Carlin

"To Kruschev, Harriman's guests 'looked like typical cap-
italists, right out of the posters painted during our Civil War
— only they didn't have the pigs' snouts our
artists always gave them.'"

— *Krushchev: The Man and His Era,* by William Taubman

"There are decades where nothing happens, and there are
weeks where decades happen."

—   Vladimir Lenin

1

"Hope is a feeling that life and work have meaning. You either have it or you don't, regardless of the state of the world that surrounds you."

— Vaclav Havel

Gob Bless America.
Dog Bless America.
And Doug Bless The America People and the New Nighted
States Of American.

"You look like you won the shittin' lottery."
Britt'ny chewed a fry and wiped the front counter.
"I did. Didn't you hear?"
He raised his voice and put a hand to his ear to offer her a hint he knew she wouldn't accept on the choice of local morning show on the radio blaring out the speakers in each corner of the building, inside and out.
"No! Really?"
The old man walked into his restaurant like he used to be somebody.
He stopped to try to read up and down the back of the T-shirt of a large red-haired woman waiting for chow.
"Yo ... outlook ... life ... result ... how ... like yoursel ...."
What? What does that possibly mean?
"How much?"
Britt'ny pressed her big stomach into the counter.
"A lot," he smiled.
He came to her, careful not to get close. He smelled almonds, maybe from the token fruit basket by the register, but suspecting cyanide in the vial she would pour in his coffee when fate handed her the chance.
"Where's my money?"

She held out her hand, palm up. She was not kidding.

"I would ..."

She stared over the heads of the customers waiting.

"Get ..."

She listed what type of car, house, land, trips, as the people waiting stared holes into her eyes and her forehead.

"Don't you want to know what I'm going to do?" he shouted from the drinks area.

He gathered his creamers, went to his closet, hauled out his broom, mop, bucket, spray bottle, pulled them all into his arms with his pop and his notebooks, pencils.

She turned away to fetch pastry, still smiling, thinking about ...

He excused himself to the front of the line, bumping shins with buckets, leaned over the counter to ask the stout girl if there were any more creamers in that box under the counter.

He stopped short, seeing she'd returned to earth.

He glared over the top of his glasses down his nose at the girl in the black glasses whose eyes just came to the top of the cash register.

He wore a yellow shirt, the same as she, red paper cap.

She smelled like makeup, he thought.

He smells like urine, he imagined her thinking.

The plump had returned to her cheeks, her eyes sunken, lips blue, not enough blood to keep everything running and rosy.

"You ... are a shithead!"

She screamed and her face glowed bright, her freckles pulsed like brake lights in traffic, her fists flat against her sides reached to her waist, no farther. She seemed to stand on tiptoes.

No, not at all, she smelled like gladioli perfume. He changed his mind.

"You don't even want it! Why do people like you get everything!"

The people in line avoided eye contact, studied the floor, looked toward the door as she turned away, seemed to be sniffling.

When actually the only thing either could smell was hamburgers and french fries, the ubiquitous hint of the dark roast.

The drivers squawked.

The old people talked loud in the corner.

But, this old recluse had no time for old men.

He hurried along, head down. He had a job to do.

Real people waiting for him.

He grabbed together his coffee, creamers, sugars, mop and bucket, broom, rags, clumped them with his pencils and notebooks and humped and clanged his way to his table, where he dropped the writing things over the table and displayed the cleaning things about as if constructing the scene for a play.

He had an idea.

That burned in his brain and in his heart, shooting tingles down his spine to his toes.

He was rich.

2

"It is well enough that people of the nation do not understand our banking and monetary system, for if they did, I believe there would be a revolution before tomorrow morning."

— Henry Ford

Gob Bless America.
Dog Bless America.
And Doug Bless The America People and the New Nighted States Of American.

The teacher ground the sentence into the blackboard with a new piece of yellow chalk, throwing flakes on her fingers and her white fluffy blouse. She rubbed her shirt and smeared the chalk into the fabric.

She gritted her teeth and clenched her jaw, then swirled back to the class, commanding them to copy what she had written on their own paper in neat handwriting.

"And tell me what's wrong."

One of the children did not hear what his teacher had said.

He sat halfway back in the middle row, smiling, with a comic book stuck inside his history textbook.

The teacher saw him. Him not taking out a fresh sheet of loose leaf paper or opening his writing notebook. Not budging at all.

He held up the history book in front of his face, with the Super Hero comic inside. He smiled and did not see the warning looks and coughs of the kids around him.

The teacher stood over him, hands on hips, glaring down.

"Can you please tell me what I just said, Mister?"

The boy folded the history book. The comic book showed on the edges.

He let the books down onto his desk like the silver revolver in the confessional.

She had the goods. She had him.

"Umm," he said.

"Will you please tell me and the class what the assignment is?"

"My favorite tree," he said, as girls around him tittered.

"My favorite vacation … and my most memorable school assignment."

Stuffed state birds — mockingbird, brown thrasher, cardinal, goldfinch — ringed the counters around the room; each state flag ran in a circle above the blackboards; each state flower — camellia, forget-me-not, apple blossom — student drawings of state sayings filled the bulletin boards.

Baggies containing state grains sat in neat rows on the card table under the windows.

Kate Smith gargled "God Bless Americans" in the intercom box above the blackboard.

The teacher wore a camo dress and blaze orange high heels with aircraft carrier earrings, framed with red, white and blue eyeglasses, and the children dressed as their favorite branch of the military.

Each child had a lunch of apple pie and hot dogs waiting in a paper sack in the cloakroom.

The class pet bald eagle perched on its post in the back of the room, pecking at the golden chain holding one leg.

The children and their teacher heard the wap-wap of a helicopter overhead and everyone hoped their grandmothers were going to be okay.

A young man with a walkie-talkie in his lap sat carefully into the rose bushes on the east school lawn.

A reporter and her cameraman hurried into the van and sped out of the station parking lot.

A group gathered by the tennis courts and softball field, drinking coffee from Styrofoam cups, making nervous little talk, waiting, sneaking looks toward the school.

Tori Francis walked her twin Malamutes down the north sidewalk in front of the school, holding the leashes in one hand and her bible to her nose with the other.

"Two creamers please, no napkin, well, sure, go ahead, that's all right, thank you."

Antoinette Marie Cole got her coffee from the drive-through. She was in a hurry, as always.

Paul Eustis, the UPS driver for this neighborhood, gal-

loped back from the Addison front door, his arms at chest
level. His goal for this day, for the entire summer: perpetual
motion.

The young boy sneaked looks at the blackboard, around
the arms of the teacher. One of his friends had crept up and
now pointed at the writing on the board.

The young boy in the wooden desk wearing the tri-cor-
nered hat made of newspaper that his mother had construct-
ed for him at the last minute smiled and looked into the dark
eyes of his teacher, back to his friend in the front nodding his
head to say, do it, do it, now! Or you're dead!

The young boy pushed up from his desk, stood in the
aisle, making his teacher move, looked out the window to
think a little more, now smiling wide.

He had it.

He placed his flat hand over his heart, proudly proclaim-
ing just before the bomb went off, "Ant to the me-public for
bitch it stands, be patient, underdog with liberty and just us
for Paul."

First they heard the snap-boom, the bark, the roar.

Tori sprinted across the lawn with her dogs tugging on her
arms.

Antoinette saw the flame and the push of the explosion
blow out the windows. She threw dollars at the cashier and
floored it.

Paul jumped in, pulled a U-turn and in a minute he
charged through the front glass doors.

The smoke cloud rose like a burnt cinnamon roll above the
school, drifting over the trees.

A police officer pushed Paul back with a firm hand in the
chest, back out the doors, onto the front walk.

A pair of emergency type persons in orange vests held up
their hands and told Tori to take her dogs and go home.

"They're gone.

"All gone," said the policeman and the orange vests.

As Antoinette jumped from her car she was surrounded by
cops pointing guns telling her to get down on the ground.

"Now!"

The group that had been milling at the tennis courts and
ball field streamed out the shuttle bus, walking fast toward
the school.

The helicopter wap-wapped overhead, someone leaning out an open bay door with a camera.

The smoke cloud floated over the neighborhoods, over McDonald's, city bank, Kum N' Go, out to the fields.

"You can't keep doing this, Zeke," said the tall young man in the red paper hat, the squeaky voice making its way through the thick smoke.

3

"Ah, fuck it. Yes! That's your answer! That's your answer
to everything. Tattoo it on your forehead! Your revolution
is over! Condolences! The bums lost! My advice is, do what
your parents did! Get a job, sir! The bums will always lose, do
you hear me? The bums will always lose!"

— *The Big Lebowski*, Coehn Brothers

"You can't keep doing this."

He looked up, into the pimples on the cheeks, chin and
forehead of the teenager towering over him.

"It's not Zeke.

"It's Harv'.

"Harvey.

"Harvard."

"Yeah. I know. Don't you think I know?"

"Yeah, well …"

Justin slid into the booth across from Harvard, in the front
window of the East Avenue store, next to Wally World, across
from the National Guard Armory, over the parking lot from
Super One Foods and Super One Liquor Store, Chu & Kar-
lee's Pizza and Mall Mini-Bowl.

Harvard Finn wore his red paper hat just barely over his
grey hair, his yellow shirt, black pants, hanging loose on a
thin frame, with all the required buttons and peppy sayings
loosely attached.

In front of him sat his three-ring notebook surrounded by
an assortment of sharpened and broken pencils, sugar bags,
creamer bags. And one button he didn't have room for that
said "I'm Really, Really Liking It."

He wrote, as he always did.

He was supposed to be cleaning.

"I've told you this before. If you are going to work here, you have to do some work. C'mon, man."

The manager looked over his shoulder at the stout girl in the yellow and red uniform, her eyes just peeking over the cash register.

Out the side of the register one saw a hand with one french fry and the hand and fry disappearing behind the register, then returning, another fry, another. The eyes never blinked.

"I'll lose my job, man. I've got dogs to support. I'm all signed up for junior college next year. I need this job. I'm starting my future, soon, man."

He pulled the notebook over.

"You know you're driving Britt'ny nuts," Justin muttered.

Harvard grinned thinly, not wanting Britt'ny to see.

He wrote "nuts" on the cover of his notebook.

Justin twisted his neck to see what Harvard had written.

"You need to read it out loud," said Harvard. "That's what they say. I never do. That's what they say."

Justin began again, out loud.

He held up the page in front of his face.

He read loud, so that everyone in the place looked his way.

"Gob Bless America!

"Dog Bless America!"

Harvard reached for the paper.

"Justin, not like that."

Justin pulled the paper away and kept going.

"And Doug Bless The America People and the New Nighted States Of American.

"The teacher ground the sentence into ... ya-da-da.

"It's good, said Justin, scanning the rest and handing the paper back to Harvard.

"You didn't really read it."

"No, I did, I skimmed. I don't really read that much."

He pointed at the notebook.

"Sure, go ahead," said Harvey.

The wunderkind manager ripped out a clean sheet of paper, grabbed one of the many pencils rolling around the table and leaned low over the sheet.

He finished and pushed it to Harv.

Harv ran his finger down the list, silently mouthing each word ... *sweep*, mop dining hall floor, sweep, mop bathrooms, sweep, mop kitchen, clean dining hall tables hourly or as needed (underlined), clean windows daily (one star), pick up parking lot.

"Yeah, I know," said Harvard.

"Just sayin'," said Justin as he got up to go.

Harv took Justin's list, crumpled it, tossed it under the table where it rolled up against a month's worth of lists, glared out the window at his bike chained to a metal pole, both tires flat, covered in snow and frozen to the cement.

It was nice of his nephew to give him this job.

Otherwise he'd be staring out the window in his room, eating soup kitchen chocolate frosting with his fingers.

Justin had thought, well, also his mother told him he had to … but he also figured, that having a jolly old guy at the restaurant would be good for business. Harvard would be someone who would joke with everyone, maybe have coffee with the old people, hand out balloons to the kids, stuff like that.

When Justin saw Harvey for the first time since Thanksgiving a long time ago, he kicked the box of balloons under the front counter.

Harvey was more of a skinny clown with grey hair that he wore in a little ponytail. But the ponytail wasn't long and daring. It was so short you wondered why it was there.

But Harvard did use the red and yellow rubber bands.

All Harvard wanted to do was write his stories.

He came in, all in a hurry, bent over, not saying hello to anyone, carrying his pencils and notebooks, grabbed a coffee with handfuls of creamer and sugar and headed for the last booth on the right, overlooking the drive-through, the highway and the National Guard.

Harvard searched his pencils for the least pedestrian.

He bent over his paper, then sat up, shaking his skull for an answer, a word, a concept.

He saw the head out of his side view, peeking around the next booth. He was used to people staring at him.

Sometimes they wanted to talk. Lots of times they just wanted to look.

"May I see?" said the pretty little head.

"See what?" said Harvard still staring hard at his papers, his pencils, his broken bicycle, wanting to give up.

He had thought about getting up to clean.

"I would like to see what you have written.

"Do you mind?"

"Sure."

He reached over the tale to hand it over.

"May I sit down?" said the woman's head.

"Yeah-yeah, sure," said Harvard, beginning to clear a space, tidy up, sweeping crumbs to the floor.

He made enough room on the table for her arms and her bag next to the full spray bottles, pencils and notebooks.

He crumpled a creamer bag and saw another on the table he had missed.

She pushed aside the broom, squeezed around the mop in the bucket.

Out of habit, Harvard immediately placed her into a story.

She was pretty, young, flirty, enthusiastic, tallish, erudite, counter-cultural, dressed in a realtor's costume.

He asked her name as she read the Gob Bless, Dog Bless.

"Hope?" she said, barely pausing to look up.

"May I?" she reached for his notebook, catching his eye for a moment, then pulling it to her and beginning to slowly flip pages.

She closed the book and pushed it with both hands toward Harvard.

"You are good."

"Really? No. I'm not. Please. Don't say that."

"How do you know that? Nobody knows who I am. Nobody reads my stuff."

"How could they? You're not special merely by being reclusive. Your duty is to get your work out there."

She folded her hands, so long and strong and perfectly on the dirty table in front of her, making good eye contact.

"Harvard, isn't that English?"

"Yeah, it's English."

"I mean British."

"No. I doubt it," he said.

"Actually, it's French, for warrior," she said.

"No kidding," he said.

"Why do you write? she said.

Harv met her stare for a moment, then gave up, choosing instead her shoulder, the ceiling, left to the ice cream cone prints on the wall, right to the people gathered around tables, talking.

She remained, waiting.

He pushed his stomach into the table edge and felt the bite. He folded his hands, tighter than she, with white and pink splotches.

"I have to," he whispered and felt his jaw quake.

His teeth rattled and it scared him. Maybe he *was* crazy.

"Look at me," he said.

She had not taken her eyes from him.

He pulled his red paper hat down to his eyebrows, trying to hide, perhaps.

"I … need … some … thing … to do," he whispered, barely getting it out. His throat seemed to be closing off. He grabbed for his drink and tipped it full up, drops diving into his dry throat.

He had not had someone sit this close and really look at him since the All-State insurance man how many years ago was it?

And this Hope girl, woman, was so pretty.

He did not smell hamburgers anymore. He whiffed whatever smart, pretty, young women smelled like nowadays. Not gladioli.

It made his eyes water.

"It's the revolution, and I have to do it."

Now his fucking eyes gushed, his goddamn nose ran, and he feared his teeth would crack themselves.

"I need it. I have nowhere else to go."

"The revolution?"

She knew what he meant, he could tell, but she wanted him to say it. Her eyes and her mouth made delicious movements, licking, batting. She wanted him.

To tell her what she already knew, to hear it spoken, out loud.

"You might volunteer, somewhere," she looked out at the cold lot.

Harvard's heart sank. He had lost her. She was gone. He was terrible. Writing was so stupid. He had to become interested in cleaning or die.

"But that's not who you are," she returned to him.

"You were meant for more."

He grabbed her around the waist, leaped from the window ledge by the drive-through, and they flew.

4

"Every time there's a revolution, it comes from somebody reading a book about revolution. David Walker wrote a book and Nat Turner did his thing."

— Mike Tyson

The next morning Harv glided through, right behind an old couple, dodging inside without touching either outer door.

Again, he was smiling.

Britt'ny watched him with amazement, her hands on her hips.

"You won the lottery again?"

"Again," he said. "I'm on a roll."

"What's with that?" she planted one hip like a stage dancer.

Harv touched the 3D glasses he had decided to wear to work that he had saved from a movie probably quite a long time ago when he had been that promising young reporter who he knew was going to save the world, and would have, if only something had not gotten in his way.

"Number 4!" came a squawk from somewhere.

"Coffee!"

"Fries up!"

"My burrito?" the first one in line whispered.

Britt'ny glared, turned and fired her wet rag at the wall and waddled fast to something, leaving a starving breakfast line to watch the whistling Harv in his red paper hat, yellow shirt, and magic glasses gather his pop mix, collect his mop and bucket, broom, spray bottles and clean old rags and head for his booth.

Harv, Harvey, Harvard arranged himself at his booth like a chicken on a nest, making everything just so. Soon creamer dust, wrappers, notebooks, pencils rolling back and forth packed the table, and the back corner smelled like Pine Sol.

Harvey liked to tell himself that the clean smell was worth a couple points. Whether it was or not he assured himself he did not care.

He opened the blue cover notebook he had purchased at Wally World, one of a pack, red, green, blue. He found a pencil and leaned low.

In the speaker above him the two hosts of the local morning radio show carried on their whatever.

"Hey, hey!"

Britt'ny cranked it, he could tell.

"Let's hear from just the rich kids out there this morning! We want you to call in and tell us what you want for Christmas and what you got last year."

"Yeah, we're tired of hearing about BB guns and wooden ponies. Boring."

"If you are wondering if you are wealthy, no need to call."

Harvard wrote, wanting to finish what he had started last night. She hadn't said she would be here, but she might.

"We've got our first caller."

"So, young lady what did you get last Christmas, if I might ask."

"A red Ford-150. Very red, almost cherry. Like candy. Shiny. Pretty nice, okay."

"New?"

"New.

"I wanted more money for clothes, but I didn't get it."

"And what about this year?"

"The new style, I guess, maybe money, probably get some dumb gifts, too, gloves, socks."

Justin slid into the booth, opposite Harvey.

"So."

The radio show switched to a sex joke and then Viagra commercial.

Harvey kept his nose down, trying to push the pencil along a line meant for elementary school children.

He smelled cigarettes and coffee and grease. He felt the thin, hard pencil and squeezed, sending his hate and fear into the wood, the lead. He made words. He thought. He shot his eyes toward the page in laser light, invisible, strong, deadly, showing the way for the hate-and-fear packed-pencil, moving, moving. To not move was to have to remember. Keep moving.

He heard the radio show and Britt'ny talking loud on the order mic, felt the cold from the door, and Justin playing with the empty creamer packs.

"These cost money," said Justin.

"They come in boxes of five thousand. You know that? Little freakin' brown boxes, a whole truckload. They're shittin' little frikking things, but they cost money."

Harvey pinched the pencil, curled his cold toes inside his airy tennis shoes, pressed his teeth together, took a deep breath. He wrote another word. He printed, tried to write plainly, even, clear, but it was sloppy.

"How we doin' on the ol' list this mornin'?" said Justin.

Harvey's chest bulged and he sat up, looked across at Justin.

"You still got my list? How's it lookin'?"

Harvey reached for it with his foot, felt a crumpled ball. That might be it.

He shook his head just as Justin grabbed for the notebook. "You got a pen?"

Four pencils rolled around the uneven table.

Justin grabbed one, flipped the notebook open, found an empty page and again spelled out the cleaning list, complete with underlines, stars, CAPS, boxes, and arrows.

He flipped the notebook around and slid it to Harvey.

"You're killing me with this. You know, right?"

Harvey watched him leave, swerve to pick up creamer cups and wipe a table and there she was standing in line at the french vanilla cappuccino.

He heard the radio clatter and rolled his pencil between his hands and watched her, waiting, moving to the front, filling her cup.

He looked down to find his place, listening.

The hard steps on tile brought her to him.

She dropped into her side of the booth like Harvey's sister at the breakfast table over Corn Flakes.

"Whatcha got?"

She smiled, brought her drink to her mouth with both hands, keeping watch over him.

For one moment he looked into Hope's brown eyes. They

grew brighter, her teeth whiter and her smile wider as he stared.

He looked away, down to the work.

He turned, flipped up, back.

He crossed out, turned it around toward her, pushed it over with one hand, careful as a curler.

As if removing the detonator from a bomb she pulled the notebook toward her through the creamer dust.

She pressed her handprint into the Styrofoam cup, held a breath and looked down.

"There was this guy, see?"

She read the story, alone in the booth, drinking her coffee, keeping her eyes on the page, while Harvey walked around the restaurant with plastic bottles in both hands shooting sprays and dabbing tables here and there.

"Please," said a white-haired woman sitting with her friend having coffee.

"Can't you see we're still here?"

"I'm sorry," said Harv.

"This must your first day. I'm Val, this is Bev."

Hope turned the pages of the story about the man in his thirties who hated his job but kept going because he had to, what else would he do?

"No," said Harvey, sitting down with the two older women.

"I've been here for months, at least."

He looked around for an answer.

"You have good light over here."

"Yes, there is," said one of the women. "Now, just what is your position?"

"Are you the manager?" said the other. "The owner?"

"No, I clean."

The women looked at each other and moved their hands and drinks to their laps as Harvey sprayed and wiped their table and their blouses.

They watched him as he moved around to the other tables without saying a thing as the old men and women raised their hands as if it were a holdup as Harvey sprayed everything.

"There was this guy, see."

Hope read the story about the young man who lived in a big town somewhere, in an office and did not like it, but he

28

kept coming to work because he liked his wife and children and house and boat. And he liked the feeling of being connected to the world, of fitting in, even though the world was all wrong, headed the wrong way, doing the wrong things. It gave him great comfort to be a part of it. To not be a part of it would be death. He knew that, and so he parked his car in the same spot, reported to work at the same time, said hello to the same people, did the same thing, each day.

And breathed a sigh of relief as he sat at his chair that he was with others, no matter where they were headed.

Harvey had never been in this part of the restaurant, all these tables, these big windows that he was actually supposed to be cleaning.

A whole new world.

So bright over here. He couldn't get over it.

He wiped the windows on the front doors, making the people wait to get in, then saying nothing as they glowered at him on their way toward the front counter.

"It's the right thing to do," the guy in the high-rise office told himself as he got onto his computer. "For family, for retirement." He went to his usual websites, political, some perhaps seditionistic, if that was even a word.

Harvey banged his mop bucket through the men's restroom door and could not believe his eyes. Papers everywhere, mud, smudges, dried urine.

"Everybody! Leave! Jesus Almighty!" he said, chasing the guys out by raising his arms into the air as if he had found a coyote in the chicken coop.

The guy dug into his pocket for a quarter. With the very tips of his fingers he hovered it in the air, examining it, smelling it, then letting it go, like a host into the mouth of a communicant, into the slot in the giant pink piggy bank surrounded by the family photos, making a solid chink.

Harvey banged out of the men's restroom, his paper hat just hanging on, his grey hair stuck to his forehead with sweat. He looked at the door for the women's restroom and kept going, plowing his mop and bucket through the waiting line.

"What got into *you*?" he heard Britt'ny as he passed. "You finally decide to do something?"

He kept going, sucking air, pushing ahead as the people jumped out of the way like frogs on the bank, the sound of the news show on the TV in one ear, and in the other the sizzling in the kitchen.

The fairly young guy in the grey suit was going to quit. He knew it. Some day. On that day he would join the people, his old friends. It would be a huge deal and people would talk about it and he would get pats on the back.

He would do the right thing and it would be a good excuse to get away from here.

All Win-Win.

Harvey stopped his cleaning caravan up close to the beverage counter, got his plastic cup and ice and filled it with three kinds of soda. He downed it and then another.

He turned and did not see the stares of the blood thirsty throng waiting behind him.

Again he shoved through the frogs and heard a faint Britt'ny admonition.

He backed his cart through the double outer glass doors and into the open air that chilled him now that he had sweated through his yellow shirt and red paper hat and his now dark blue underwear.

Harvey left the cart on the sidewalk right in front of the door. He stumbled around the parking lot, painfully bending over to pick up hamburger sacks and apple pie boxes. He found himself way on the other side with his hands full of shit and nowhere to put it.

The man in the thin brownish hair pushed back on his glasses and sat back in his swivel chair, staring at his computer screen. Feeling a tingling in his arms he made fists at his sides, pushed off on the carpet in his black shiny shoes to the very middle of his cubicle that he shared with two other men who were not there yet.

Harvey approached his dying bicycle chained to a post, touched the front tire with the toe of his tennis shoe, and let himself be distracted by the hard plastic red garbage can where he stuck the shit clutched in his hands. He looked in and saw her, still sipping her coffee, tiny, distracted sips, without looking, reading his story.

Now Justin hovered over her holding the glass coffee pot. She finally looked up, smiled and held her cup for him.

"Go away! Git now!" Harvey screamed inside his own head.

He relaxed a bit when she looked down forcing Justin to slink away.

Harvey perfunctorily made his way back to his cart, filling his hands again, as nine people scrunched inside the outer front door area waited to make their way, one by one like prison escapees, around the cart, with mop, broom, bucket, rags and two holders for spray bottles.

The youngish man in the grey suit and the thin brownish hair slumped in his chair in the middle of the largest cubicle on that end of the floor, his feet stretched straight out, ankles crossed.

Both of his cubicle mates walked in together, laughing. They saw him and began sneaking and snickering, whispering.

One reached to pick up the guy's glasses on the floor and the other thumped him on the back of his head with his finger.

5

"Those who make peaceful revolution impossible will make violent revolution inevitable."

— John F. Kennedy

Harvey banged up to her, every contraption on his cart clacking, squeaking and complaining.

She waited with her crushed coffee cup trapped inside her folded hands.

His closed notebook waited for him at his spot.

The radio in the speaker right above them played oldies at low volume.

He sat down, winded from his twenty-minute cleaning adventure.

She smiled at him, not as big as before, then looked over his shoulder at some exciting traffic.

She hates it, hates me and she's trying to find a way to let me down and get out of here, he thought.

Oh, well.

With one shallow breath he accepted it.

It was only a tiny hop from the flying ledge back into a room with a TV.

He had already found the channel changer and pointed it.

"I think it's interesting, the revolution."

She made air quotes that curled his toes.

"I went online. Ha. We were watching basketball, do you like sports? I think they're just okay."

More air quotes.

He made a move to answer but she kept going.

"The kids were still making noises, outdoor voices indoors. I had my laptop on the couch, sometimes that's all I need, you know."

He nodded as if understanding.

"That's like the '60s? '70s?" she said.

He shook his head.

"Isn't it?" she said.

"Like what Jefferson said, like every once in awhile, you know, umm."

"Thirty, twenty maybe," Harvey mumbled.

"Anyway," she said.

She thinks it's trivial, he thought.

To him it's vital, like breathing!

The Goddamn Revolution.

It almost happened. I don't know why it didn't. It just didn't. But now it really will, and the only reason I know that is because it has to. It has no other choice. Nowhere else to go. It's all in a goddamn corner!

Then something in her eyes switched.

She lit a fucking cigarette!

"This is the revolution," she said as she blew out the smoke. "I know, right?"

"Right."

You can't do that anymore lady!

He wanted to shout at her and raise clenched fists at the same time.

"Who are you?" he asked as she ashed into her open hand, wishing he had not opened his mouth. He was so stupid.

"I'm like you," she said, ashing, puffing, as Harvey felt a thousand eyes on his forehead.

You cannot smoke in here, lady. Not even pretty people.

He heard police sirens, fire engines, radio announcers.

The rising smoke gave them away, their position, their stance.

Over here, shoot us first.

"I want to make a difference. It's what we all should do. Isn't that right?" she said, ashing in a cup.

"I really don't think I have any choice," he said.

"I have to write."

"But it's also the *right* thing to do."

She made air quotes with one hand.

"Kind of a nice coinky-dink, huh?"

"Oh, coincidence, yeah," he said.

"Yeah, yeah, I guess, maybe. Yeah."

"Restlessness is an itch that ends in progress," she said. "Somebody said that, not me."

You just did, Harvey thought. That's all I will remember.

"You can't deny DNA," she said.

"There are reasons for it. The survival of all.

"There is a reason for you," she whispered, leaning forward over the table and showing more than Harvey thought she might have meant to, but maybe not.

"Well, thanks," he said.

6

"I really do inhabit a system in which words are capable of shaking the entire structure of government, where words can prove mightier than ten military divisions."

— Vaclav Havel

Nobody wants to do too much, really.

Pull the picnic table into the street and surround it with the deck chairs and the lounger, haul out the rifles and shotgun and see how long it takes until the police kill you in front of your dog? Twenty minutes? Half hour?

And then what you did was make everyone think you were crazy and plant that picture in everyone's heads that it's something nobody wants to ever do, ever again.

Thanks to you.

But to think that anyone, even people in Detroit living in abandoned buildings or farmers getting tossed off their land by a guy in a suit driving a green Camry, would go to that kind of trouble.

That's a stretch.

There's always their phone and TV shows, find enough money for a pizza, couple beers, and things aren't so bad for tonight and that's all you have to get through is tonight.

Harvey sat in the library reading the paper he used to work for, not really reading, skimming for something that made sense, trying to think of something more to write. Today he was not inspired. Today he was going to quit.

He might die soon, but when? When? See, that's the deal. That's the whole deal right there. He could kill himself. But how? And shit, that was not cool. Somebody would care and then it would be what Harvey had done to that person. He couldn't just quit, stop moving, give up.

You think about it.

How would one go about it? You still have to piss, to shit, you're breathing, you get hungry, thirsty, might as well eat, take a drink. You get cold you want to be warm. You get tired you want to lie down. You want things. Even after you give up, you want things, want to be satisfied in ways.

You could just plop down in a chair and say that's it, I'm done, get somebody else. And then in a few minutes you got to go pee, and it escalates from there.

In the practice it's just not that simple.

In real life maybe you sit there all very depressed, as all hell. Nobody loves you. Nobody knows about you. You are never going to be famous.

Nobody's going to read that crap you spent all this time on, and not because it's some Russia law on writers, but 'cause you are a fucking joke. Never going to be a big deal or even make any difference.

What you are is somebody's dad, someone's uncle, someone's crazy old son sitting in a little house and then apartment and thinking he was leading the charge, when he was just doin' a hobby, like whittling.

He'd just been making a spoon from the big tree out back, all this time, and wanting the folks to want to each have a look and hold it at Christmas and nobody really caring about another old wooden spoon.

And all this time thinking he was dangerous.

Over the years every once in a while you think like this, but then some little asshole says he likes your stuff and you act like the little a-hole owns *The New York Times* and *Newsweek* and so you keep working, doing your thing and for a while you are excited about it and one day it's like somebody threw water on you and you did not realize you were sleeping.

And that's why you're sitting in the corner, your legs splayed over the little chair that is the best in this room but not great, and you are done, over.

Maybe you cry.

Maybe you feel like it, but you don't.

And then, goddamn you, you get some spark of an idea in your fucking head and you throw your legs over the chair arm and reach into the garbage for the notebook with onions and shit all over it. You wipe the ketchup and sauce shit off the pencil and you find a flat spot somewhere and you write down that stupid fucking little sprig of something that had come into your stupid fucking head and you just *had* to save it.

If you'd let it go, it would be gone, down to the bottom, and you knew it.

You knew it and you chose to save it.

You stupid, cra-zy old fuck.

But, well, there it is, and it seems there are words that might go with that stupid fucking little shit phrase or clause or whatever those words mean you scribbled down in your sloppy retarded handwriting like some fucking guy a hundred years old with Alzheimer's, cancer, gas, a hundred other whiny things, trying to scribble down "milk, bread and soup" on the inside of a frozen pizza box he has decided he wants to fuckin' use for a grocery list.

Well, yeah, fuck it, you are writing again and you keep kind of going, in between pissing and finding some bread in the pills drawer and staring out the window at some cool little bird that you don't even see because you are all inside your head and this little piece of shit thing you are doing in front of you.

And like maybe a couple of hours later you snap out of it, like where was I?

Inside you're all smiley and a little hungry and you grab your rag coat and go for a walk and wave at the first motherfucker you see like Santa Claus leading the goddamn Christmas Parade.

7

"I freed a thousand slaves I could have freed a thousand more if only they knew they were slaves."

— Harriet Tubman

"That's what I want! That's what I want!"
The little boy pointed up at the movies, top row.
"I … want that!"
His mom reached up and grabbed "Charlie and The Chocolate Factory," and toted it again to the counter.
At home the little boy sat up close to the TV as his brothers and sisters made noise and wrestled behind him.
He saw how poor was Charlie, living in that little run-down home and the grandparents living in the bed in the middle of the living room and Charlie's parents so poor and good-hearted and doomed.
The movie ended and his brothers and sisters all lined up like Choopa-Loopas to dive into the river of chocolate, and pretend they were right in the movie with Charlie with the golden ticket.
This Charlie ran to get his gun, black plastic, silver sights with "John Dillinger" right there on the handle.

Harvey inserted a "writer's note" into the text, anything that might make him different, noticed:
"I used to hope for this, what we have now, dictatorship, censorship, to help my writing. I would be like Solzhenitsyn, Tolstoy. I would be special because of the censorship. If there were not censorship, then what was I talking about?"

The news people said nothing about it, what he had done, John Brown.
As they said about many things.

38

He called himself John Brown, but it could have been anything, anything at all as he walked into the bank as he had walked into the insurance agency yesterday and pointed the gun at the face of the first person he saw.

He demanded money.

"Now!"

And they hurried, scrambled, fell to the floor to bring it to him faster than possible.

"Boom!"

He shot at the last person he saw, the big bank man, not big sideways, but tall.

His white shirt grew red, redder, reddest.

His knees thumped together and his head cracked open on the tile floor.

"Welcome to Wally World."

Said the big woman with the faux blonde hair, longish, just brushing her broad shoulders.

"That's the last one," said the giant man next to her.

Ten large people with chains and padlocks stormed the glass doors and wrapped the doors and connected the chains and locked the locks.

"That's it," said the large woman.

The giant man nodded.

"Nobody gets in or out 'til we get our money."

"Action."

They raised their fists into the air and walked to the back of the store to the wall of giant TVs to see if they would be on the news.

Notes:

How the rich think. They think in advance. They think they want to have money and they figure out how to have money. To them money is not evil. To them poverty is evil.

How the poor think. The poor think backwards. They wish they had money. They don't know how to get it. If they get it, it will be by luck. They don't think they are lucky.

"I'll never be able to spend all my money."

That's a rich person stating a fact. He made that happen. He expected it. That's how it is.

"They're just people. Take care of yourself, your family."

That's a rich person telling another person about poor people.

"Hang on!" she screamed back over her shoulder.

The teacher turned the bus, yanked the wheel, it squealed, on two wheels.

She was driving the bus, as usual, on the tour, the school trip to Mount Rushmore for the fourth graders.

She's the fourth grade teacher. The fourth graders always go to Mount Rushmore for the school trip in the spring to celebrate the year being almost fucking over.

Not today.

Not today.

This time they go some place that means something.

This time they are going to see where the Indians were hanged, to where the young blacks were shot in their beds, to where ranchers hunt down poor people in the desert, to where government snipers killed people in their own home in the woods.

8

"Not being heard is no reason for silence."

— Victor Hugo, *Les Misérables*

She skimmed with her finger down the last page, closed the book and pushed it back.

"Okay," she said.

"Okay?"

From her jacket pocket she pulled a folded color brochure and handed it over.

"I swiped it, from the library bulletin board."

She smiled.

"The Valley Region Writer's Gang," he read out loud.

Meeting Thursdays, 6 p.m. at The Whole Table, he read in silence.

"A writer's club," he said.

"Group," she said.

"You'll be able to get tips, meet people."

Harvey got up, walked to the restroom, picked up a couple of paper towels, stared out the front window, heard details of the coffee conversations he didn't want to.

He walked back and she was still there.

"You could learn."

I feel like I should, yeah. I should join this coffee book club, and learn, and meet people, and laugh and have a good time and not be depressed and a burden and so serious and not in touch.

But I'm not going to, go to, no goddamn book group meeting and read my paragraph and ask them if they like it.

Ask them! Ask them?

And then have to talk about wild rice soup while the next person finds her glasses that are big as airplane engines, fit halfway down her nose and her husband there in his casual clothes that cost more than my apartment for the summer. And then listen to whatever crap she writes.

And even if it's not crap, I don't care.

I'm in it for me.

I am this writer. They are them.

I am the best, the most important. I am going to change the world, put the President in the street and push the Pentagon into the river.

I am going to do all that and I have not been working on this for how many years to go humbly sit in the back table of some whole grain restaurant and mumble for an hour and say we'll come back next month and do it all again, and that's fine?

While the world burns? While my ass burns? My head, my stomach!

He thought all that, staring a hole into the table, sensing she had gone.

9

"Listen, the next revolution is gonna be a revolution of ideas."

— Bill Hicks

"The world needs you. The world does not read.
"The world does not read because it has never read you.
"Write. Write. Write.
"Leave the rest to me."
And so now she was this … this, literary agent?
Harvey drank coffee from a red and yellow Styrofoam cup with both elbows on the table, looking over the top of the cup at Hope talking like an Apache at a wagon train blinking with neon lights and a marquee.
What happened to the goddamn book club? The wheat bread. The mocha grande, ten percent off for club members, during the meeting time only.
"Why didn't you tell me before?" he asked.
"You never asked."
She tried to smirk-smile out of it, but he would have none of it, but still, a real agent?
"I run into writers, like you, all the time," she said.
"In this town?"
He looked back over his shoulder, up over her shoulder at the line, the steam in the kitchen from shit frying.
"And, on email, conferences, everywhere.
"Well, anyway, if you are committed to making a difference, I can help you. You have a lot to offer."
Harvey bowed his head as his boat sank, bow and stern.
"Two-hundred fifty dollars," she said.
"Then we can get started."
"You are already a big success."
"Really?"

43

"Yes, to have gotten this far, with all your writing. Most don't get to this point, but I need a show of commitment from you to make it all work."

"You need money," he said.

"Yeah, seems like that's how everything works. It shouldn't.

"But, it does, unfortunately."

10

"The revolution is not an apple that falls when it is ripe.
You have to make it fall."

— Che Guevarra

Harvard sat at the big table.

The Tuesday night candlelight meeting.

He'd already introduced himself to these people he'd
known for twelve years.

He held his small head easily in one hand and scribbled on
the pad in front of him. Everyone was used to him doing this.
He wasn't taking notes, just doodling, pinching the pencil
tight, in order to breathe in, out.

"They're covering the graffiti they say in this New York
subway line, the murals. They say it's to clean things up, but
that ain't it."

Harvey listened.

"It's the power," a woman said.

Harvey looked up.

"Of art," said the leader of the meeting way down on the
other end.

People wagged their heads.

These are not ordinary people, thought Harvard.

These people.

People only revolt under imminent danger.

If something smells clean, it smells clean.

The group home, the hospital.

His sister, Justin's single mom.

Harvey doodled and held his head while everyone talked.
He liked to sit on the one end where this group leader always
started.

"How about let's start down there tonight," he would say every time, and Harvey could get his little speech out of the way right away.

In the low light, with little candles scattered around the long table, he saw his paper and the shadows around the room, and he had about an hour to think.

And if he got a good thought, something for a story, he had his paper right there.

If it was still a good thought and not stupid the next morning, then maybe he could fit it somewhere.

People only revolt under imminent danger.

If something smells clean, it smells clean.

The group home, the hospital.

His sister, Justin's single mom.

Tonight it was just thoughts he could not really turn off after giving his little speech, the little speech that should be routine by now, but each time it's kind of a big deal.

Harvey took his magic glasses from his red and yellow uniform front pocket. He touched his head and felt the red hat. He put on the magic glasses and nothing much happened. The coffee cups and ashtrays turned two shades darker.

He shook. His knees, his jaw.

The reason for choosing Tuesday night. The candles, low light.

Sometimes he was fine, laugh, say some things, repeat his lines, fit in, hold up his part in the play. Pat backs on the way out, say have a good week, see you next week, huh?

This was not like those Tuesdays.

He was supposed to be forgetting things at his age, letting some things go. But it had seemed for a time that those days of then were right up with him now, pushing him, insisting he remember and so smug that he was unable to do anything about it.

Suffer you son of a bitch, the thought daggers said.

People only revolt under imminent danger.

If something smells clean, it smells clean.

The group home, the hospital.

His sister, Justin's single mom.

Harvey kept his pose as he had trained. Head in one hand, doodling with the other. So cool, so detached, just bein' cool.

Sometimes he pissed his pants on Tuesday nights and had

to leave before the leader got up to turn on the long overhead lights.

Harvey waited, tightened everything he controlled.

He sat in the dark in the basement of the corner building of 2nd & Commerce, wearing his magic glasses in his red and yellow uniform, pinching tight, gritting his teeth, holding on, trying not to fall apart.

Some day it will happen. Some day, but always he fought it, not today.

He doodled, pushing the lead into the paper, through the paper, through the table, the floor, into the earth, piercing the heart of the earth because it was crying and it should not suffer.

And there goes a couple in a car moving down the highway. The man drove. The woman sat in the passenger seat. For a while they did not talk. They took turns messing with the radio, correcting the others mistakes in tuning, in regulating the heater.

She stared out her side watching trees fly by. He glared at the road, the line in the middle, the lines on the sides. He scowled at the cars in the rearview and threatened the one he was approaching.

Something must be wrong.

They went on this way for miles, then for an hour.

He thought all the reasons why he was angry and did not like her and she fired back those thoughts at the same time.

He did not like his job. He wanted to quit and he wanted to do something that he liked.

She thought back at him they had bills to pay and a list of things that came into her head and she threw at him, smashing him and all the big things he thought he was into a thousand pieces puzzle. ...

Harvard stopped with his writing to listen to someone, and also wondering where he was going with this little story about the man and woman driving. What did it have to do with his stories?

He put a ... where he had left off in case he ever figured it out.

And that made him sad. If the thing he was writing did not make sense, he was sad, depressed. If it made sense, same thing, only opposite.

47

He thought about his school story. Where he had left it with Rori, no, Tori, Antoinette, and Saul.

"They're gone. They're all gone," he wrote.

The group moving over from the tennis courts, the smoke clouds drifting over the town, the helicopter, all the emergency personnel rushing toward the school.

He thought about the morning radio show he was forced to listen to every day at work.

He put them into his school story and had them tell everyone over the radio that all the children were killed by the bomb.

He put into his story people who did not believe what the radio station men said, about the bomb in the school, or airplanes disappearing into holes or other things the men on the radio station said.

That is the revolution, he wrote.

Knowing of what is bullshit and telling all the people.

So much revolution.

As much revolution as in that unplanned moment when someone meets the stare of a policeman and does not look away.

Too much.

Too much knowledge and the world will explode in joy and agony.

He turned the page and made a list of unhappy people, types of people, not real people. An unhappy teenager. A couple sitting in a movie and sitting through six awful previews of violent movies that they don't want to see. But they take it. They are afraid and they take it.

Afraid that if they make a scene or shout the rest of their day will not go as well. If they sit and just be silently mad for a little while, then things will be okay. The unhappy teenager was registering for the draft. And the people in the car were talking about paying taxes or not paying taxes. And the wife wants to have children. She is pregnant, see?

But the husband, well, he's all panicky because he will never be able to do what he wants now. People with children do not fight on the barricades. He actually said that to his wife when they started out driving that day to get out of the house. And she said, the barricades? The barricades? What ... the ... *fuck* ... is a barricade?

And there is this armored car driver.

All those bags of money.

He's got a gun, right there.

And he knows just as soon as he wakes up every morning with this new great job he just got, that the only person he has to really be afraid of is him.

If he does not take that one step he will forever have his life, his coffee, his pillow, those comfortable jeans, his shows, his new puppy that will one day be a big dog.

He pushed on the rickety door, kicked in the dark to find the first riser.

Harvey tromped up the steps, straight up.

Wooden steps. Wooden handrails, both sides.

He slid his hand along the one.

The smell of 1930, the smoke of cigars long gone, laughter and heartache and factory work and jitterbugs embedded in the wood.

He entered through the door off main street. A door that you would not know was there unless someone pointed and pointed and then walked right over to it and touched it. There it is.

The long hallway lay dark and silent.

He swiped off his hat, ran his fingers down the wall and over the doorways.

His particular wooden door from the '30s lay halfway down, one up from the community toilet.

Harvey felt the familiar loose brass knob and pushed the door of his American home open. He flicked the switch with his elbow and the bare bulb in the middle of the ceiling said hello and that's all it said.

His room held a bed, a chair, a window, a small table by the bed with assorted necessities. The tiny closet was empty. An extra shirt hung over the back of the chair.

He sat in the chair and looked out the window, tossed his notebook at the bed.

Should he pay her?

He should not pay her. He should quit, just quit everything. Stay in this room until his rent was far overdue and then go walk around, walk as far as he could go and then somehow it would all end finally.

Maybe she can do that.

49

He did not get up, but slid to the edge of the old wooden chair, leaned it on two legs, reached the notebook with his fingertips.

One last thing, he thought.

And then that's it. I've done enough, too much. I should have quit ten years ago, nine.

Oh, it's been fun.

This one will work.

Hope.

He smiled wide and looked down onto the headlights of two cars passing on main street and the one more coming from way over there.

11

"You'll get pie in the sky when you die."
— Joe Hill

"Hello!"

The door swung open and the words came out before the black-haired woman stuck her head around the corner.

"Oh.

"Well.

"Come in then."

She disappeared behind the door and Harvey was left to look all around at the pretty home.

She pulled a chair out quickly from the dining room table and ran out of the room.

He sat and heard banging of doors and spoons clattering, and then it stopped.

He smelled coffee. He looked around, at the photos of Justin and his sister on the bureau, of his sister and her husband, arms around each other, smiling like tomorrow or yesterday were not days on the calendar.

She returned staring hard into the cups of coffee in her hands, set one down in front of Harvey, another over there and then she sat, began to drink, look down into the coffee, as if there might be a hair waiting to bob up and she wanted to pick it out.

The clock ticked and the coffee around the corner dribbled while melting snow from the roof plopped into a puddle in the frozen flowers.

Harvey scanned the room for more photos, parents maybe, he and his sister, that one with them in a leaf pile. He twisted, checked the ceiling, the floor, then twisted back.

"You dye your hair," he said, knowing right away, he had

...

She touched it and stared hard at her coffee.

"It looks good," he said.

"I really like it."

She looked at him as if discovering him in a box of Cracker Jacks.

She smiled.

He smiled.

He reached a hand out to touch hers, to hold her hand, to squeeze it, and got as far as his thick white coffee cup. He squeezed it, fondled the handle, rubbed it.

"I was wondering," he said.

So he asked for the money.

She actually growled, looked as if she might be getting sick.

They sat in silence. The coffee stopped dripping and the outside plopping ceased since the sun was gone.

She pushed off from the tablecloth with both hands as if resolutely refusing pumpkin pie offered too many times across the Thanksgiving adult big table.

She returned with a checkbook and pen, set to write without asking how much.

Like a bowler slowly with both hands flat ripping off the score sheet to go pay after a fun night, she laboriously tore out the check and set it on the table where he needed to get up to reach it.

He picked it up without looking closely, folded it, put it in his uniform shirt pocket, pulled his red hat down tighter.

"You were expecting someone?" he said.

She fell into puzzlement, grew more thin, her nose longer, her skin grey, the grey also showing through at the top of her scalp.

"When I came in."

He twisted to point at the door.

"You were smiling."

"Yes," she said, as she got up to follow him, she assumed he was leaving, and just so, so he was.

"Thanks," he turned and patted his chest just as the door whooshed closed on his nose.

12

"There were twenty-three CIA agents waiting in a conference room for me. I counted.

"What stunned me when I first walked in was — these people looked like "the neighborhood." I mean, some appeared to be in their early twenties, right out of college, alongside what looked like sixty-five-year-old grandmothers. Men and women. It was very diverse. As I looked around at them, I thought, there's the lady down the block you see sweeping her front step in the morning, and wave to — 'Mrs. Jones, how are you today?' Just an average middle-class neighborhood. Except they were all with the CIA."

— Jesse Ventura, on a meeting held after he was elected governor of Minnesota, from *Don't Start The Revolution Without Me*

"I got it!"

Harvey pointed at the bank envelope in the middle of the table before Hope had a chance to sit and get settled in.

"Oh, that," she said.

"Well, okay."

Well, okay? he thought.

She counted it inside the envelope.

She pulled out a form, flipped it to Harvey and pointed with her nice pen where she had already checked the boxes showing what she was now obliged to do for the money he'd given her.

"Well, okay, then," he said.

He reached to shake her hand as they stood.

She took it and smiled.

"Good luck to you," she said.

"To us both!" Harvey smiled wide.

He sat back down, opened his notebook, found a good

pencil and watched her walk way across the parking lot as she always did, to the white SUV waiting way over there by the Dumpsters.

13

"I am convinced that the truest act of courage, the strongest act of manliness is to sacrifice ourselves for others in a totally non-violent struggle for justice."

— Cezar Chavez

I'm alone.
I sit alone. I sleep alone. I eat alone. I walk alone.
I am alone.
Maybe that is the way of the revolutionary. The rogue wolf. Maybe that's how it has to be, but I don't really think so.

More like with all these other revolutions and there were a bunch of guys doing it together. There weren't a bunch of people each setting up a single barricade on all these different streets.

I don't fit in.

I've tried lots of times to squeeze in and fit. It has never worked, so I just assume it doesn't.

I'm not saying it's a great way to be. I'm just saying that's the way it is with me. Not that it's great. I'd rather have fun. Wouldn't you?

I think you sort of get what you deserve.

And I don't think I could really kill in a revolution. Maybe. But I don't think so. In a way it might feel good to kill somebody really bad or really rich and to be able to think, yeah, now, that's better.

But when you were killing them, or for a long time after you wouldn't be able to think of them as rich or really deserving it, at least I don't think so.

You'd think about their face when they were dead.

14

Well, the folks in town
They dress so fine
And spend their money free
But they would hardly look
At a factory hand
Who dresses like you or me

Well let them wear
Their watches fine
Let them wear their gems
And pearly strings

But when that day
Of judgment comes
They'll have to share
Their pretty things

— Natalie Merchant, *Owensboro*

Why write this? These stories.
Because I can make it happen.
If I don't write it, it won't, it can't.
That's how it works. There are always writers that come before the real big stuff that gets all the attention.
Always?
Always.
And people will be finally free of having to do stuff they don't want to just because they have to.
And they will have more things that they need, and they will be happy, and they won't have to feel trapped, and not so sad anymore.

15

"The greatest challenge of the day is: how to bring about a revolution of the heart, a revolution which has to start with each one of us?"

— Dorothy Day

Harvey tried not to think about Hope every day.

He tried so hard that's all he could think of.

He did not know how long he could hold off Britt'ny and Justin, and his sister, with their stares and their glares and their little remarks, enough to crush the revolution, send the revolutionary to Siberia with a roll of the eyes.

"So, how's it going?"

Britt'ny stopped by the table after the morning rush.

Harvey looked right through her. He knew now exactly who she was, what she was. He could read her like the dollar menu, small and cheap.

Britt'ny left and then Justin waltzed up.

They had the dance all worked out, thought Harvey.

They are good.

Justin sat down.

He leaned over the table and said, like just between us guys.

"You know, I know you don't care for Britt'ny so much."

He sat up.

"She ain't so bad. She just wants you not to lose your job, that's all. She says, and I agree with her on this one. You might want to start emptying the trash. It's starting to build up a little."

He put up his hands like Harvey had a gun on him.

"That's all ah'm sayin', ya know? That's all."

Harvey stopped writing to look up at Justin.

Justin leaned forward again, getting very close to Harvey.

"Hey, how's uh, you know, with the *agent*, ya know, and all that, huh?"

He started to place air quotes and stopped.

They were digging for info, thought Harvey. First one, then the other, fat cop, skinny cop.

Well, it ain't gonna work.

"Pretty good," he said.

It had been three weeks, two days and he had thought for sure Hope would have returned by now.

But he wasn't going to let on.

No sir. No sirreee.

He still had some gas in the ol' tank.

Two more weekends dragged past.

Then two more and another three.

Harvey wrote at his table, stared out at his dead bicycle outside the restaurant front window, right by the drive-through.

Every five minutes he sat up to look for Hope's white SUV over by the Dumpster.

Two more weeks he looked out his window at the cars going past, at the seagulls diving at the city trucks scooping up the slush into dump trucks and hauling winter away.

His money was gone.

Now he knew it.

He had known it three weeks ago but now he really knew it.

One more day, he thought, and then I quit. I'm not doing this no more. No more. A little bit more! And then that's it.

In the dark he spread his hands out like an umpire making the safe sign.

Then he crawled up under the rough blanket, curled his knees to his stomach and stared at the street lamp shadow wall with big eyes.

The next morning he bounced in the front door like he had just won the lottery for the third time since he had passed retirement age.

He flashed the peace sign, grabbed an apple, took a bite, tried juggling a banana and the bit apple, winked at Britt'ny, grabbed his cleaning stuff, his coffee, and whistled the tune from the closing scene of Les Mis', which he had listened to last night through the walls or the window of his room.

"They got that out now on DVD," said Britt'ny to the next customer. "Musicals blow, you? You wan' a drink with that?"

Harvey Finn sat, wrote.

All morning the local radio show shouted down from the speaker just above his head. He looked for her vehicle all day long.

Justin stopped by to talk, then left.

Britt'ny set down a fresh drink next to Harvey's notebook.

He nodded his head in thanks and sipped at the straw, silently acknowledging she had gone to the trouble of mixing the lemonade, Dr. Pepper and Orange Crush.

Justin slid into the booth and slapped drum noises on the table, smiling, apparently trying to get Harvey's attention.

Harvey looked up.

"Hey, man, maybe you got some time to clean today, huh?

"Hey, just kidding. You know I'm kidding. I'm a kidder. That's what I do. That's why people like me, right?"

Harvey nodded and stuck his nose back into his notebook and tried to make the pencil move.

Justin popped out a closing drum beat, boo-pop-a-loo-bop, beep-beep-beep.

"You keep going writer man," he said, holding up a clenched fist.

Harvey looked up once more as Justin walked away in one of his long strides, reaching back at the last moment to reach out a long arm and shoot Harvey with his hand gun.

Between the eyes.

Harvey leaned low again, pushed the pencil into the paper, making a dent, snapping the lead.

Harvey stuck his hands into his pockets to warm them and stood that way, artfully escaping the booth. He walked to the front, around the stainless steel front counter, aimlessly, like a visiting nephew at Thanksgiving.

He walked around the kitchen, hungry, smelling the hamburgers and fries. He weaved his way back, into the wilderness behind the ovens, past the whispering cooks and owls in the dark, back up again toward the light and drama and glitz of the drive-through window.

With his hands in his pockets he watched, smiled at the young girl working the window, nodded to a guy about his own age in an old red pickup, waiting for his sack of dead meat.

The other guy just stared, hard, wanting that hamburger and cherry malt, his one hand over the wheel, the other working the cigarette from his mouth over a broken window, around the cold.

And getting it.

Harvey watched how the old guy his age maneuvered the cigarette and the battered construction worker hands, the window, the sack, the money rumpled into submission, set the bag somewhere, pulled the gearshift down into first and never said a damn word to the big dog on the passenger's seat sitting there like the wife who came along just to see people.

The scene made Harvey realize he wanted.

Not the truck, or the food, so much, but the big, unsmiling dog.

He wandered more, toward the front door, now carrying a broom, dragging it over the floor, staring out the window at the cars. He listened with his back to the coffee drinkers. Maybe there was something there, something he could be a part of, join, sit down and be somebody.

He waited, holding the broom, feeling the cold air through the window, and moved on, trailing the broom behind him.

Harvey came to the children's playroom, an enclosed area with some colored seats for the moms to rest and the pool of red, yellow, green and blue balls where the kids would swim, dive, jump, hide, laugh.

Harvey looked around.

He went inside, sat at a yellow table. He looked around some more.

He slipped over to sit on the side, his feet hidden inside the balls.

He let himself down and stood waist deep. He fingered his grey hair behind his ears and sat, just his eyes above water. He moved his arms and feet back and forth inside the balls. He dropped back, rolled around under the balls, flipped to his stomach and crawled. He came up, shot up and dived back down. He probably looked like a porpoise swimming he imagined.

Some people walked by and he ducked down, imagining himself a secret agent on a dangerous mission. He dived deep, crawled along the bottom and came up in an entirely different area than an enemy agent might have imagined.

With praying hands, down again he want, throwing up a wave of red, blue and green balls in his wake.

He did the breaststroke, spreading the dimpled balls from his path with his hands and kicking them away with his feet. Harvey hit bottom, a plywood sheet.

He read. "It is not possible to live but for someone else."

He pushed the balls away, but they filled in immediately.

He shooed them away, seeing something else written over there. He went to it, positioned his behind and his back to make a space so he could read, shoving balls away furiously with both feet, wrenching his back and his neck to be able to read:

"Be bold and watch mighty forces come to your ... ."

He dived into the balls, scurrying along the floor, leaving a wake above as if a gopher were making a home. He chased the balls away, brushing, scattering, looking for more of the writing, but found nothing.

A woman came in, holding the hand of a little girl, then turned and walked to a table.

Harvey climbed out of the ball pit on his hands and knees to the little yellow table to pull himself up, left through the glass door, tried to smile at the woman and the little girl who were having none of it.

The rest of the day he sat by himself at a fresh table away from his rolling pencils and notebook, a table free of creamer dust and torn bags.

With his back to the noise of the restaurant he stared out the back window, past his defeated bicycle in the slush, through the melting drip from the roof.

He thought of how he was not exceptional.

He was regular, normal, nothing more.

There had been others before him.

He had not even taken time to write something pithy of his own on the ball pit plywood floor. It had been done.

And the ancient ball pit writer was right. This was not possible alone. It meant nothing.

Harvey was totally alone and it was not possible to live that way. You must be able to do what you do for some one, with some one, or you can't do anything. Things done totally by yourself, for yourself, are empty.

Nobody starts a revolution for themselves.
"Oh, I wish you were there."
"I want to tell you about something."
"Did you see that too? I thought about you."
At five o'clock his hand smacked the glass door and he pushed out into the chill. He walked across the parking lot to the pizza place. He ordered and sat atop the free papers on the bench by the window.

Hope stormed in, bringing the cold air to Harvey's ankles, right up to the counter, in a hurry, ordered in a shout, presumably to make her pizza bake faster, stalked right over to sit next to Harvey.

She breathed hard, trying to catch her breath.

"Hello, Hope," he said.

She looked to him, then to her pizza.

She continued, as if all part of the plan.

"It's not going well," she said.

"By definition this isn't going to work out for you."

"By definition?"

"It's just not. Unless you are willing to really put yourself into this. You have talent, Harvard. What you need now is commitment. Are you willing to go the extra mile? There are a thousand, ten thousand just like you, who can write as well as you. What are you going to do, to stand out. That's what it boils down to, in the long run.

"I need a little more incentive, you know, to make it work. We are close. This close. I'd do it for free, if I could. You know that."

She put her fingers together up by her nose.

The pizza boy called her name.

On her way out she turned to Harvey.

"Let me know what you want to do."

16

"Credit complications in the check out line
It's an awkward situation almost every time
They keep your card behind and they keep your groceries
too
Yeah they do
You try telling everybody it's a terrible mistake
 But you can tell they don't believe that's true
It's written all over you
When you're broke
By the time I got home I was seeing red
I pulled the gun up out from under my bed
I put a sock on my head and into the night I flew
 Away I flew …
 The next thing I know I've got blood on my hands
 But I've got money in my pockets too
You never know what you'll do until you do what you do
When you're broke

— Todd Snider, "Broke"

Harvey Finn sat in his chair, facing the window.
Something clawed at his door.
He opened it.
The black and white cat walked in, hopped onto his desk.
Together they watched the cars go past.
"They" let you go on and say whatever you want as long
as you are small. This eliminates a lot of work for them, as
well as feeding the myth of free speech. Little guys talking out
and their people would say, well, we do get to say everything
we want, so I guess … But, the trick is, as soon as someone
starts to reach a large number of people or have an impact,
that's when they will be shut down, stomped on, stuffed into
a sack and thrown away."

Harvey talked to the cat, Hampton.

He closed the door, telling the cat again about the water in the Styrofoam cup on the floor, and that he would be right back and to keep watching for him out the window.

On the sidewalk Harvey backed way up to the curb to see up to his window to see that Hampton was looking, but joking as if he could not see Harvey.

He walked, in and out of parking meters, his red cap on backwards, yellow shirt untucked, pushing the raging forces in his brain against each other into the final battle.

If he would be famous and change the world, then he would be rich, but then he would become what he said he hated. Maybe he could be rich for a while, do some things, then give it away, sell the condo and the boat, move back into his room.

That is exactly what he'd do.

He felt good about that.

He watched for Britt'ny and Justin out driving around. They probably watched him, knew where he lived, knew all about the cat called Hampton and already the Styrofoam cup with "Hampton" in pencil, cut in half.

Harvey turned sharp left off main street, sat on a bench next to a bar.

He's CIA. The President is CIA. She's CIA.

I have never met anyone in the CIA. I have lived for many decades. I have never seen a CIA agent, even in the most ludicrous, smallest town Fourth of July Parades, or even on TV.

So, how can I say, she is CIA, he is CIA, this is what the CIA does. They will do this, they will kill you, take you away, trick you, make you go away.

The truth is.

I just don't know.

Sometimes I think I know. I wish I knew.

Some people say they know and so then I say what they say and then think that I know too.

I just don't think I know.

Anyway, not that much.

Not everything.

Not some things.

Not whether the CIA, FBI is over there, or there, or coming here.

It would be nice to know.
That would be pretty cool.
You would know a lot more things, if you knew, that.
Maybe I'm right.
But I don't know.

Having done his due diligence, Harvey got up and continued on his quest.

The armies charged, on foot, on horseback, swords raised, mouths wide, pissing themselves, eyes glaring, shitting themselves on the run, soon to clash, mesh, to become one, to vanish, to become sawdust and daisies.

"No. Nooo. No!"

The screams escaped the front door into the neighborhood just as it slammed.

Harvey walked fast down the front sidewalk, away from his sister's house, in one motion throwing open the gate and almost shutting it behind him.

He clomped down the street, shoelaces flapping, arms high for speed.

He heard her behind him. Soon she would have him and at least it would be over.

Harvey's sister overtook him.

She threw her arms around his shoulders and he stopped.

She turned him, hugged him, squeezed him.

She took his hand in hers and led him back to the house.

Inside, in the foyer, Harvey Finn waited.

She hurried back, clattering over the stone floor.

She handed him the envelope from the one hand and the gun from the other.

Harvey's sister explained that the old revolver was their father's, that he kept for emergencies.

"Oh, I see," said Harvey.

He had always wondered about that. One of those things he had never gotten around to asking because that felt better, the not quite knowing.

"I decided I don't want it," she said.

"Oh, okay," said Harvey.

He stuck it into his pants, felt the cold steel barrel hard on his testicles and felt dangerous

17

"It seems obvious, looking back, that the artists of Weimar Germany and Leninist Russia lived in a much more attenuated landscape of media than ours, and their reward was that they could still believe, in good faith and without bombast, that art could morally influence the world. Today, the idea has largely been dismissed, as it must in a mass media society where art's principal social role is to be investment capital, or, in the simplest way, bullion. We still have political art, but we have no effective political art. An artist must be famous to be heard, but as he acquires fame, so his work accumulates 'value' and becomes, ipso-facto, harmless. As far as today's politics is concerned, most art aspires to the condition of Muzak. It provides the background hum for power."

— Robert Hughes, *The Shock of the New*

"I cannot believe you gave that skinny bitch more money!" Justin stood at the urinal next to Harvey.
Harvey made good time by not washing his hands.
He slammed his palm on the door, hearing Justin punching the roaring automatic hand dryer and swearing.
Harvey made a circle, from the cleaning closet, around the coffee groups, to the women's restroom, put out the yellow sign in spanish that he didn't know what it said, and sat in the women's can, smoking cigarette butts he had found outside on the way in that morning.
Clattering like a clown car Harvey pushed through the busy lunch line with his cleaning supplies as Britt'ny interrupted a woman ordering the No. 4 to put her hands on her hips and stare.
That evening, before dark, he sat at his window with Hampton on his lap aiming his pistol at cars and people on the street.

He put the gold ball on a young man's head.

"Phshew!"

Harvey sang to Hampton as he set the next empty can into the line on the table.

The head exploded.

"Bsheepow!"

The gas tank on the silver SUV blew up, spewing fire and shrapnel through the jewelry store and bakery front windows.

Harvey reloaded, popped the top on the last can and rested the barrel on his arm to begin his assault on the used music store.

Click, click, click, he fired and ducked low under the window ledge, then reached the gun up and fired blindly to hold them off for a while. He pushed his back up against the wall to reload, sitting on the floor, facing the door.

Hampton sat on the bed, its head in its paws, watching Harvey the outlaw, the rebel, fighting against all odds with nary a chance of victory, still fighting, a warrior.

Harvey placed his hands flat on the floor and raised his chin to the ceiling.

"Armored cars and tanks and guns, came to take away our sons, but everyone must stand behind, the men behind the wire!"

Hampton stretched and walked to the edge of the bed to see out the window.

"And a rain swept, hmm, hmm graveyard … was where he was laid!"

Harvey yelled.

"You only have a deep-seated desire to think more of yourself than others as a consequence of having a low self esteem!"

He shouted it word-for-word. He remembered. He fucking remembered. All that shit.

"What does that mean? What does that possibly mean!"

He tipped back the empty can, way back.

"Gerard Casey! Will never be forgot!"

Harvey swept his cup from the table as he reached to get up.

He knelt and aimed his gun out the window, stuck the pistol into his pants and tugged at the pane, his face red, still singing.

Knuckles rapped in the hall.

Hampton jumped to his shoulder.

His face covered in sweat, his face red, his chest heaving, his shirt running up his stomach, Harvey carried the gun and the beer and the cat to open the door.

The two policemen knocked him to his back, flipped him to his stomach, handcuffed him and dragged him down the hallway, down the steps, banged him through the old wooden door and out onto the street.

"Who sent you?" he asked them when they all got situated.

"Justin and Britt'ny?"

Harvey ducked to look up as they yanked away from the curb to see Hampton watching, putting a paw on the cold window as if to wave.

Harvey slept in the holding cell.

He went to court the next day and was sentenced.

"Dude! I know you! You're the guy from the restaurant! Like that clown dude, that hamburger dude! Dude! I know you!"

Harvey walked into his block carrying his grey blanket, pillowcase and baggie holding his toothbrush, toothpaste.

For ten days Hope was absent from the restaurant as the radio station played in the speakers, Justin did his paperwork in the little office behind the ovens, Britt'ny fought with the customers and the old people pissed away their lives and the decaf.

18

"In my son's veins flowed the blood of Irish rebels"
– Ernesto Guevara Lynch, Che's father

Harvey Finn sat at the yellow table.
A round yellow table bolted to the concrete floor.
The table stood in the middle of the dayroom.
Across from him sat a young man. They wore orange head to toe.
Harvey leaned low with a pencil above a single sheet of white paper. The yellow-haired young man hunched like a crow about to devour a nest of sparrows over a similar sheet, gripping a pencil hard in his fist.
Harvey leaned on his pencil, not hearing the TV, the talk, the nascent arguments, the squawks in the intercoms.
He was The American Prisoner.
He was dangerous.
The time had finally come and he was the one placed in this position. He was danger, like the famous ones and the ones who will soon taste fame.
These around me are the poor, the oppressed, and I am here to release them from their misery, to lead the charge.
Like Luke he would take everything they had and keep going ... he would be the best, the worst, the famous, the most famous.
He would never give up.
At the next table over sat another young man in orange, with deep black hair to his shoulders.
The blond-haired young man drew Super Heroes killing cops, with bullets, laser beams, fists, bombs, tanks.
Every now and again he twirled the page and asked Harvey to look.
"That's good," said Harvey, wanting to have someone to sit with.

The black-haired young man played solitaire. He was new to the block, just came in last night. His hair and collar looked as if he might still be drunk.

After taking a look at the Super Heroes three times Harvey felt the right to talk a little about his work.

But first he went to get coffee for them both in tiny Styrofoam cups.

"Hey, Harv," said the guard who had just come on duty.

Harvey nodded.

"None for me?" said the black-haired young man, keeping his eyes on his game.

"So, why?" said the young artist. He crossed his legs, kept his eyes on his paper.

"Geronimo and shit."

"Huh?" said Harvey Finn.

The young man looked up, straight at Harvey.

"Why would Geronimo do it?"

"Do what?"

"Fight! You know!"

"Well, isn't it obvious? He had no choice," said Harvey.

The young man looked down and nodded.

"Lenin, Castro, Guevara," Harvey said and he'd already gone too far.

"Ho Chi Minh, Washington, Franklin, Havel, Walesa."

"Yeah, them guys, yeah," said the young man, looking up for a moment, pointing his pencil at Harvey and then back down to his battle scene.

"Dow-dow-dow," he mumbled to himself, drawing dot-dot-dash-dash tracer bullets.

The black-haired young man smiled and scooped up his cards, began to shuffle, laid out a new game.

"We own you."

He almost laughed, smiled big to himself, as if remembering the night before.

"Why?" said Harvey, leaning across the table.

"Because I see and I know and I understand and there is no one else or way or time. Because of you and I feel it and I have seen some things and heard stories and read some things, and my father would be proud, I think, and his father, and when I see them they would shake my hand firm and perhaps smile. I feel things and I have to."

The black-haired young man laughed out loud, keeping his eyes to himself.

"You don't really know, do you?" he said, flipping out three cards, three cards.

"If you really knew you could say it in three words, not a hundred, you old fool."

Harvey and the young blond man looked back at the young black-haired man.

Then back to their little talk.

"And well, these are my people.

"All that stuff."

"My people," the black-haired man said, getting up for coffee, laughing.

"What stuff?" said the young man at Harvey's yellow table.

"What I just said.

"Oh, I wasn't really listening.

"Say it again."

"No.

"I can't.

"I can't remember all that. You should have listened."

"If you can't remember, if you can't say it again, well, what's that say?

"Dude, just sayin'.

"Should you really do this?

"Start the world on fire, ya know. I heard some, ya know, not that much. You hungry?

"Maybe you should join an old folks home."

"You don't join. They have to take you, accept you. Anyway, I don ..."

The black-haired man slapped the cards on his table.

"Maybe you should apply. You might get lucky, Clown Man. You don't know until you try, right?" said the young man drawing with Harvey.

"I know, right?" said the young black-haired man.

"We fucking own you."

"Then why are you in here, dude!" said the young blond man, firing a tracer finger.

The black haired young man looked eye to eye with the blond man.

"Minor setback, son. I'll be out of here by the end of the day. You, dude, will never leave. It's like all-a 'at."

No don't, please, don't, Harvey thought as the young man at his table produced a pointed metal something from somewhere. His eyes bulged and shined red, his face and necked blotched as he pulled himself in slow motion up and away from the table.

He rushed at the black-haired young man and lunged the last few feet over the table, one hand on the shoulder, the other throwing the homemade knife into the heart.

Harvey swirled around, got up, took one step forward then shuffled off, away, behind the next table.

They toppled from the table, slamming the concrete. In a few moments the young blond man had stabbed the black-haired man a dozen times in the chest.

An alarm sounded over and over like a fire truck trying to get through heavy traffic as the unit guards dived on the blond man and guards pounded from every direction in the hall and into the unit.

Blood spread across the shined cement.

Blood covered the face of the young blond man, and the smirking dead young man beneath him. Blood covered the bare arms of the muscular guards and their crisp blue shirts.

Guards rammed the live young man to his stomach.

He fought them, looking for Harvey, kicking, butting, punching, doing everything he could to get one hand up and show Harvey the peace sign.

They got him cuffed behind his back and pushed him toward the door, his feet only now and again touching the cement.

He kicked and threw his head around.

They dropped him again and Harvey heard a thump like a melon or a brain being crushed against the concrete.

"Revolution!" he screamed as they pushed and pulled him out the door.

"Harvey!

"Harvey Revolution!"

On the big day Harvey walked out of the unit and into the concrete block room painted puke green that was heaven in the mind of every prisoner. St. Peter and Jesus handed back his red hat, yellow shirt, magic glasses, black pants, white tennis shoes and let him out the side door.

He nudged into his old room with his elbows, his hands full of hard, free rolls from the morning soup kitchen.

"Hampton!" he said, just as the cat sprang from the room, down the hall out the front door that Harvey had propped open with a new small-sized cat food bag.

Harvey rushed to the window to see Hampton dash into the street and be struck, right over the back, the stomach, gushing, exploding, by two wheels of a white SUV.

There Hampton lay, in the middle of the street, stuck to the pavement, legs outstretched, eyes bulging.

Harvey walked to work with his gun in his pants, carrying the half bag of frosted flakes, knowing that as soon as he left his room would be padlocked.

"Where you been?"

Justin and Britt'ny met him at the glass door.

"Umm."

Harvey tried to sidle around them.

"You got to move your bike, man," said Justin.

"And, you can't sit here anymore," said Britt'ny. We've got to get someone else."

"I can't be doing this," said Justin. "They're making me manage another store and this one."

"One more," said Harvey. "One day.

"Just let me sit, please? Just one."

"No," said Britt'ny. "You really, really need to get out, Harv."

"Five o'clock, man, you're history, man," said Justin.

Justin moved, a little.

Harvey squeezed between them.

He sat at his table, with the mop and bucket and broom on display, the creamer packets, creamer dust, his coffee cup, pencils rolling, hunkering over his notebook.

19

"Every morning when the hiring boss blows his whistle, Jesus stands alongside you in the shape-up. He sees the family men worrying about getting the rent and getting food in the house for the wife and the kids. He sees you selling your souls to the mob for a day's pay ... And what does Christ think of the easy-money boys who do none of the work and take all of the gravy? And how does he feel about the fellows who wear hundred-and-fifty dollar suits and diamond rings, on your union dues and your kickback money? And how does He, who spoke up without fear against every evil, feel about your silence? You want to know what's wrong with our waterfront? It's the love of a lousy buck. It's making the love of the lousy buck — the cushy job — more important than the love of man! It's forgettin' that every fellow down here is your brother in Christ! But remember, Christ is always with you - Christ is in the shape-up. He's in the hatch. He's in the union hall. He's kneeling right here beside Dugan. And He's saying with all of you, if you do it to the least of mine, you do it to me! And what they did to Joey, and what they did to Dugan, they're doing to you. And you. You. ALL OF YOU. And only you, only you with God's help, have the power to knock 'em out for good."

— Fr. Barry, *On The Waterfront*

The little boy had grown.

He was still Charlie.

He drove a mint con-dish woody station wagon that his grandfather gave to him the day before he died on the line, the checkout line, at Wally World.

Charlie commanded a hundred men who lived in bare rooms and in tents out by the river.

The little plastic gun with "John Dillinger" etched on the

barrel was now an automatic known to every bank teller in two counties.

The newspapers called Charlie "The Terror," and asked people to turn him in, put his picture in the paper every day, gave money for tips on his whereabouts.

The local morning radio show called him every name in the book. They made jokes about him, talked about where he came from, his grades in school, his mother, his father, his sister.

"We beg you, Charlie, come in here," they said over the air. "Come in here, you coward, you bum, you loser. You hide, you talk big, you say all the big things, but we don't see nothing. Come in here, right here. We'll put you on the air, talk to the people. You'll find out real quick. People laugh at you, Charlie.

"They laugh.

"You are a coward. You are an insurgent. You are nothing but a dumb kid from the east side and that's all you will ever be."

Charlie ate chocolate for breakfast, every morning, because he could.

He never gained a pound.

It was a Tuesday.

A Tuesday morning, in the summer, yeah.

Charlie tore through the town firing back out the window with his guns blazing.

They were everywhere, all around him.

He stopped for the light, and then he thought t'ell wid it, and he gunned it, just as a black and white cop car vaulted through the intersection.

Charlie never saw what hit him.

He flopped into the middle of the street.

The two cops shot through their windshield, smacked their heads open boom-boom, almost at the same exact time, on the old maroon bricks of the hardware store on the corner.

A woman ran into the street and dragged Charlie away.

They searched for him, for that woman, the rest of the day, but they never found either one.

No sir.

Three days later fire engine horns, tornado whistles, cop car sirens and all the church bells in town rang and blew all day long, just like they'd been doing ever since those two cops hit their heads on the hardware store and the woman got Charlie outa there.

Charlie woke up in a tent on the riverbank with the woman kneeling over him dabbing at his face with a washcloth.

Helicopters thumped along, following the river.

"It's no use," said the woman.

"You'll have to give up. Tell your men to go home. It's over."

Charlie knocked her to her back with a swat of his blood-stained arm.

He called for a meeting.

"Tonight, midnight."

They huddled around a campfire in a cave in a bay in the woods along the river.

All the hundred were there, seated and standing all around, smoking, pitching rocks sidearm at the river.

They listened to Charlie and then they sang deep into the night.

The next morning, just as the first school bell clanged, and the workers in the bank and the offices had just sat down to rest with a hot cup of coffee, a black and white police car sitting empty in front of the station, its motor idling, erupted, jumping as high as the roof of the station house and crashing to the ground blazing, shooting smoke around the whole downtown.

Fourteen of Charlie's men stormed the bank downtown, thirteen more took the branch at the mall.

Four snipers on rooftops picked off one at a time — ping-ping-pow — the policemen and firemen who tried to put out the scorched black and white cruiser.

Over on the other side of town, as the parade was just beginning, pulling out of the parking lot next to the football field, Charlie himself rode a bicycle, carrying a blazing torch like the Statue of Liberty right toward the color guard leading the parade, as it began its way through the west side, toward the ceremony in the city park.

Before the soldiers holding the flags knew what had happened they held burning flags, still marching, still leading the mayor's car, the apple pie float, and the high school band through the big yard part of town.

Charlie raced back, clutching his torch, peddling his stolen bicycle, raising it high above his head, the signal for those hiding in the bushes behind the people lined up to watch the parade to flick their lighters and set ablaze the perfect piles of leaves in the front yards.

A giant stack of fiery military camo uniforms, caps and boots in the first intersections blocked the path of the parade led by the burning flags.

The blazing leaves caught fire to the yards and bushes and homes, leaving the backyard pools isolated pleasureful oases.

Just before the homes went up in smoke Charlie and his men snatched the apple pies from every window.

From the top of the press box in the baseball stadium three of Charlie's best men squatted with shoulder-held rocket launchers.

As the fighter planes and bombers making their ceremonial run over the town streaked low, Charlie's men knocked them from the sky, pushing the shattered hulks into the big homes and the swimming pools and the motorhomes and Mercedes.

Charlie stood on his red bicycle to pedal extra hard, headed for the radio station, his gun stuck loose inside his pants.

A police car, lights flashing, siren blaring, slammed through the intersection sliding, spinning, blocking his way.

Charlie threw the handlebars back and forth and beat it instead for the city park, sweat flooding his eyes and his arms, screaming loud to get there faster, not wanting to miss it, to be part of the toppling of the statues and the destruction of the cannon.

20

"Let every dirty, lousy tramp arm himself with a revolver or knife and lay in wait on the steps of the palaces of the rich and stab or shoot their owners as they come out. Let us kill them without mercy, and let it be a war of extermination and without pity. Let us devastate the avenues where the wealthy live as Sheridan devastated the beautiful valley of the Shenandoah."

— Lucy Parsons

Harvey Finn looked down.
He had finished writing.
His notebook sat closed before him.
The table was cleared of debris. His mops and buckets, broom, spray bottles, waited to be returned to the closet, hoping for someone new to put them to real use, so, so tired of being patient.
Harvey felt the five o'clock shadows around the big room. The slow-down of movement that lasted eight minutes precluding the evening rush.
He heard Justin and Britt'ny spraying themselves drinks from the fountain, scuffling across the dirty floor, snapping towels at each other, giggling.
Saw their shoes, toes inside of canvas, wiggling, nervous, anxious.
He stared at the closed notebook and the pencils in a row, all facing the same way.
The drive-through squawked, traffic whooshed past through the highway spray.
"It's time, Harvard," said Justin.
"It's over."
Harv touched the gun in his pants, took a deep breath.
"We have it!

78

"We have it!"

The muffled hollers penetrated thick glass, growing louder as Hope clomped across the parking lot, through the outer glass door and then the inside door.

She tapped across the tile, both hands in the air, papers flapping.

She stopped at the fountain, took a big breath.

"Mind?" she looked at Justin.

Britt'ny stared. Justin stared.

Hope grabbed a large cup, filled it with ice, then orange, root beer, lemonade.

"We got, we got it, we got it."

She spilled a bit, kept going.

She hustled up, in front of Justin and Britt'ny to stand over Harvey.

"Got what?" said Britt'ny while Justin made clattering and banging noise gathering the cleaning supplies.

"Really?" said Harvey, wondering what they had got, almost having forgotten what he had been waiting for all this time.

Hope slid into the booth opposite Harvey.

She spread the papers out, slurped and dribbled on her chin, sucked it up.

"It finally worked!

"Hey-hey-hey, what'd I tell you, Harvard P. Finn?"

"I can't really remember," he said, pulling the papers toward him, spinning them around.

He read.

"They are interested?"

He looked up at Hope.

"Absolutely.

"All you have to do is sign there."

She touched the bottom of the letter with a green fingernail.

Justin came back, sweeping. Britt'ny tried to read the papers over Harvey's shoulder.

"What?" said Justin.

"It worked," said Harvey.

"She has a publisher. I have a publisher. Someone wants to make my notebook into a book."

"You're kidding," said Britt'ny.

"No. Not kidding at all," said Hope.

79

"Harvard Finn is a real writer, will soon be a published author, that is, someone to be reckoned with, a contender."

"No longer a pretender," mumbled Justin.

"I kid, man," he pointed the broom handle at Harvey.

"Who's the publisher?"

Britt'ny leaned low over Harvey's shoulder, still trying to read the small print.

Hope grabbed the papers.

"Someone very reputable," she said. "Someone you obviously wouldn't know."

"Well, la-fuckin-tee-da," said Britt'ny, standing straight as a stump, her hands on her hips.

"You are an author!"

Justin leaned down to hug Harvey.

Justin pulled Harvey out of the booth, raised Harvey's hand like he had just won the fight and announced to everyone in the restaurant.

"My uncle, Harvard Finn, is a published author motherfucker!"

Some people waiting for Happy Meals clapped lightly then turned back to stare hard at the young man trying to work the cash register.

"Whoop-te-fucking-do," someone said.

Justin lined up Harvey, Hope, Britt'ny in a conga line and led everyone around a couple of the back booths.

Harvey's sister rolled through in her Oldsmobile outside. A cautious cat perched on her shoulder, peeking over the top of the half-open window.

She saw them dancing, scowled, then drove away slowly.

Hope broke off the line and stood over a counter smoothing out the official-looking document.

"You didn't sign, Harvey."

Her fingernail pointed at the line. You just need to sign this."

"What is it?" Justin pushed in.

"What's that?"

"It's really none of your," said Hope.

"It's just a formality," she said.

The green finger ran around the page.

"It just makes me executor of your writing, blah, blah, blah. Just a formality. It's the best, quickest way."

"Executor?" said Britt'ny, peaking her hand between the arms of Justin, Hope and Harvey.

"That's like in a will. Is this a will?"

She shoved all the way through with authority since her grandfather had recently died, put both her elbows on the counter and leaned over the paper.

"You just need to sign this, to make me the executor of all of your writing, just a formality. It's the best, quickest way," said Hope.

"Maybe executor isn't the best possible term."

"You mean I won't be able to write anymore unless you say I can?" said Harvey.

"In a way, yes, technically, but, hey, bud, we are in this together."

"We're going to the top. This is the revolution. I know, right?

"Right?"

"Well, okay, sounds good."

Harvey pushed in, moved Britt'ny out of the way, put his hand up. Hope placed a pen into the hand.

Harvey signed the paper.

Hope snatched it up.

She quickly walked out of the restaurant, holding the paper up over her head, shouting back over her shoulder.

"I will be in touch!

"You will want to acquire a better class of friends! Get out of here!

"Adios!

"Get out there and enjoy this beautiful day!"

"Do you get any money?" said Brittany.

"I don't know," said Harvey.

"Executor?" said Justin.

"You dying, Harv?"

"I didn't think so."

Britt'ny bent to the floor to pick up the silver pen.

She handed it to Harvey.

"What's the title of your book, Harvey? What are you gonna call it? What's it mean? What's it all about?"

21

"It still would be years before I understood the seriousness of my change of view. Much later, I recognized it in "Revolution," the essay of Polish journalist Ryszard Kapuscinski, who describes the moment when a man on the edge of a crowd looks back defiantly at a policeman — and when that policeman senses a sudden refusal to accept his defining gaze — as the imperceptible moment in which rebellion is born. "All books about all revolutions begin with a chapter that describes the decay of tottering authority or the misery and sufferings of the people," Kapuscinski writes. "They should begin with a psychological chapter — one that shows how a harassed, terrified man suddenly breaks his terror, stops being afraid. This unusual process — sometimes accomplished in an instant, like a shock — demands to be illustrated. Man gets rid of fear and feels free. Without that, there would be no revolution."

— Gloria Steinem, *Revolution from Within*

A placard sat in the middle: Harvey's Table.

Harvey sat against the wall watching the old people talk.

Justin slid another "Harvey's Wallbanger" across the table to Harvey.

Harvey's new, green notebook sat in his lap.

He folded his hands around the cup, nodding when someone looked his way, sitting directly underneath the speaker and the morning radio show.

Justin worked outside the window on Harvey's bicycle, a red toolbox open on the walk, tools splayed around. He smoked, sported his red hat backwards, bobbed his head to the music in his ear buds.

Harvey slid down on his hard yellow plastic bench, so that his chin rested atop the table as if he were the Christmas meal, then disappeared below the table, to his knees. He had heard, in between the coffee table chatter and the clinking of the cups, a pencil rolling around on the floor.

He pushed along around the feet of the old men, their tennis shoes, black shoes, white sox, scabs, white legs. He took a plaid slipper to the ribs and another to the jaw.

One white head showed up below the table.

"What in hell?"

"My pencil," said Harvey.

All the white heads popped out, upside down and sideways, looking at Harvey on his hands and knees.

"His pencil," one said.

"I have a pen, somewhere."

A head disappeared to dig for a pen.

"Maybe you will need a pseudonym," said one of the men to Harvey, still on his hands and knees, reaching in the dark for the rolling pencil.

"Yes, maybe," said Harvey.

"Why?"

He paused to sit back on his haunches.

A pen clattered down at his feet.

"You will be too famous, that's what we were saying. You won't be able to go anywhere, get soup, mow your lawn."

"I don't really have a lawn," Harvey whispered to himself. He doubted they'd be all that interested.

The heads moseyed back up, as one.

"Yale T. Zane," someone said.

"H. Finn."

"Yale T. Zane. I already said it. Didn't you hear me. I just said it, just now. You had to have heard that."

"Okay. Or it should be symbolic, or honor the town."

"Yeah."

Harvey found his pencil and sat on the floor, opened his notebook in his lap and set the lead against the paper, to see if he could write.

Inches above his head cups banged the table.

Harvey Finn looked up. Right above his nose, in pencil, he read, twisting his head back and forth to catch the best light.

"If one advances confidently in the direction of his dreams, and endeavors to live the life which he has imagined, he will meet with a success unexpected in common hours." Hank Thoreau

Oh, God, thought Harvey.

I give up.

Harvey dropped his head and closed his eyes.

He listened to the men talking about possible titles for Harvey's book, ideas for the cover image, book tours, and possible other books to follow.

Justin gave Harvey a ride home.

They put Harvey's bike into the trunk of Justin's Honda.

Justin's passenger seat was broken and there was a hole in the floorboard. Harvey had to lie flat, put one foot out the window and one on the dash.

It's only a few blocks, Harvey thought at just the same time that Justin said it.

On the way Justin talked about the pressures and perks of being the manager of two stores, and how he might like to some day invent his own chain of restaurants with a special theme and menu.

They walked up to Harvey's old room.

"Thanks again," said Harvey.

"No problemo," said Justin.

"Just remember us when you're famous."

Justin put the used hot plate in the open window.

"Mom's looking for a little fridge for you, too," he said.

"She wanted me to tell you."

"What's that?"

Justin pointed to the gun on the bed.

"A gun."

Justin picked it up, felt the weight, looked it over close, rubbed it.

"Make your wishes," said Harvey.

"What?" said Justin.

He aimed it out the window at the people and cars one story below.

Harvey put his hand on Justin's arm and pushed the gun down.

"No," Harvey said.

"It was my father's."

"Oh."

"*Your* grandfather."

22

"The first lesson a revolutionary must learn is that he is a doomed man."

— Huey Newton

The rain sat on Harvey's hands and nose like sweat.

He perched on his bike, leaning up against the same old metal post on the far end of the drive-through.

Hope didn't know where he lived. He didn't have a phone. This was the only place.

The rain dripped from the bill of his red cap.

He watched out over the parking lot where she would leave her white SUV and come running up.

Inside the window he watched the new old guy smiling and talking to people, sweeping and wiping.

The "Harvey's Table" cardboard thing scrunched on the counter over by the dirty trays.

Justin was mostly over at the other restaurant these days.

He watched Britt'ny walking behind the counter people, the portable phone thing on her head, directing the show, encouraging, pointing out, shouting, joking with the customers, pitching in, like a general on horseback prancing back and forth behind the front lines.

It poured now, like the whole junior high headed down stairs for lunch.

Harvey gripped the silver pole that must have been for something at some time.

Headlamps from each car turning the corner behind him shined for a moment on Harvey's back, like lights in a drive-in movie catching someone doing something for a moment.

Harvey slowly moved his toes inside his wet socks, which made him need to pee and his toes ache and sent a shiver down his back and started his jaw to quiver.

The sun shined through the clouds and rain, blinding Harry as he stared at the few parking spots in front of the Dumpster.

Harvey took a big breath, and thought of the Japanese guy he had heard about somewhere, on the internet, who lived alone on an island. He said he felt pretty much in harmony with nature, and when he got to feeling bad it was because he was making too much of himself. He felt he should be more like a grain of sand.

That's not the American way, Harvey thought, his lips flapping with the escaping air.

That's not the way I am. I want to be the wave that comes in and arranges every grain of sand the way he liked.

Maybe it doesn't matter what we do. No matter what I do, little or small, it won't matter. Nobody will see. Nobody will hear. Nobody will care.

That's prob'ly how it is.

Yeah. Yep.

Should we light ourselves on fire in the middle of the intersection, or curl up and take a nap in the one last patch of sun on the living room floor.

I won't be rich.

I won't be famous.

I won't fulfill my goddamn promise to the fucking universe.

I'll be a wad of wet toilet paper stuck to the mirror thinking it's a big deal. What's it for in the first place and when it dries out, it's even less than that.

See, *that* is fucking brilliant.

Why don't they see that?

No.

I probably can't even write. That was all bullshit.

I'm no good.

"Hey."

"Hey."

Britt'ny waddled around the corner toting a red and yellow umbrella.

She stood next to Harvey.

"How's Justin like his new job?" he said.

"It's okay, I guess.

"I'm moving to Bidgebee. It's in Oklahoma," she said.

"How come?" he said.

"I've always wanted to live there," she said.

"She wasn't that good for you."

"At least she was trying to help me," said Harvey.

"And that helps you too. It helps all of us. We need these stories! We need these stories!"

"I'm just sayin'," she said, running a hand down the back of his hand through a bunch of raindrops doin' nothing.

He pulled his hand up to look, to see if she had written something in rain on his hand.

She hadn't.

"You should come in and warm up," she said.

She walked away, ducking her head against the wet and cold, leaving Harvey trying to balance holding onto the silver pole with one hand and the umbrella in the other.

Harvey held the umbrella for a moment in his teeth and moved the gun in his pants so he could sit more comfortable.

Could he kill?

Was it worth it?

Would it be the best way?

Why him? Why did he care?

The revolutionary walks right up to the statesman at the banquet into which he has sneaked.

The statesman smiles and holds out his hand to be honored as a creepy smile forms in his head and his mouth, knowing, then seeing the knife in the copper hand as it charges, plunges, into his own stomach, and turns and churns and lets out all onto the floor, for all to see.

How does the brave, young, handsome, intelligent revolutionary feel to see the old, rich tyrant's dead eyes roll as he smashes his nose on the shiny tiled floor?

Has he ruined his own life in this instant, or fulfilled it?

Harvey leaned his bicycle against the green newspaper box by the front door. Inside the entryway he folded the umbrella and shook off like a cocker spaniel.

He came in and slid into one of the small front tables, shivering, keeping his eyes on the lot.

His teeth chattered.

The floor became wet all around him. The old men and old women stopped talking for a moment then continued along as Harvey pulled out the pistol and banged it on the yellow plastic table to get the wet off.

Britt'ny set down a smoking foam cup of coffee.

He watched her walk across the parking lot, face-first into the driving rain.

He sipped the hot drink and shivered from his hair to his toes, watching her over the top of the cup.

She went to the Dumpster, to a little yellow hard plastic receptacle.

With a not insignificant effort she threw open the red lid, leaned way inside and pulled out a blue notebook. Without returning the lid, she turned to march back, the wet wind as her sail.

She shivered the rain like another dog coming into the restaurant, two in one day, opened the second door, shuddered out loud, then placed the notebook on the table in front of Harvey, shoving the gun to the farther side of the small table top.

Harvey whispered the title on the wet, smelly cover in a hoarse whisper.

"I think you're pretty good," Britt'ny said as she turned, peeled off her red windbreaker and headed for the kitchen.

Harvey saw the tip of a pencil still stuck inside the wires of the notebook.

He reached for it, pulled his hand back.

He touched the handle of the gun, ran his hand up and down the pearl.

He snatched up the coffee with both hands, noticed the one loose-leaf sheet sticking out of the notebook. He had often wondered if it would stay or not like that.

Hmm, it had.

He stared hard over the top of the cup with his brown eyes deep into the eyes of the old men and old women at the other yellow tables, five feet away, and the corner booth, next to the extra trays and the garbage dispenser.

23

"We are sorry for the inconvenience, but this is a revolution."

— Subcommandante Marcos

Notes:
The revolution is happening.
It's not being televised, reported, written about.
The revolution is happening now.
The man read the writing on the wall, on the fire station, the library, the police station.
He nodded knowingly.
Some old people had said they were going to help him to advertise.
The man walked, with a purpose, one hand swinging, the other inside his pants.
He walked from where he was to the lights, across, to the tracks, sniffing the hamburgers and fries, smelling rain, feeling his stomach rumble, trying to picture in his mind somewhere where there was food he could have.
Seeing the world through the same eyes and heart of a young boy on the sidewalk watching the birthday party through the big front window, hearing the click of the traffic light tsk-tsking him, he plodded ever onward, pushing himself into whatever darkness or light remained.
"Toot-toot! Toooot!"
The train roared through town down the hill one block.
It clicked, clicked over the rails and ties. He stopped to watch the blur, setting it to his memory.
The man touched the pistol in his pants at hearing the invisible outside speakers of the radio station delivering the morning talk show voices to the street.
He stopped along his way to think and look around. On a

bench, in a coffee shop, where he was told to leave unless he was going to order something.

He left.

The man walked past the radio station, staring at the windows, the colored letters on the windows, hearing the morning show in the speakers.

Water drops from the awning found their way to his neck and he hiked up his little coat.

He walked into the neighborhood, up the hill.

The old neighborhood. His old house, not so far from his sister's new house.

He scuffed down the alley, kicked at rocks and bottles, some he thought he recognized, remembering something in every old garage and tree and garden.

If he would not do this.

In any case, he did not have to, and so maybe he should not.

If he did not do this, he could return here, to family, friends, smiles, the old days, new days, good days that would stretch from here to as far as you could see or count or walk.

He stopped in the middle of the alley and he saw the backyard where he had been chased away from the birthday party that he had not been invited to, pursued by all the boys and shoved down face-first into the mud, kicked and shouted at and told to leave.

He had left.

This one particular man made his way by the church, just to be walking, past the school, the hoop, the old fence.

He folded his fingers into the chain link and leaned into it, staring into space.

He pushed off the fence and it shook.

He tugged his cap down low onto his brow.

The man hesitated, then walked inside the radio station, nodded to the receptionist who had already smiled.

He sat in the chair by the window with the magazines and the little table and the coffee.

She asked if she could help him.

He shook his head and felt the gun barrel pushing into his leg, probably make a big round mark.

Some men in one's and two's stopped by the receptionist to say one or two or three words and leave, nodding to the man over by the coffee.

The man saw the plaques and pictures and flags on the walls in this big room and also down the halls.

He got up once to walk to a plant to smell it as if that was what people do. It did not smell and he returned to his seat.

He got up to leave and left without saying goodbye.

The man walked down the sidewalk, now feeling out of rhythm, confused, afraid that he was something he had hoped he was not, some thing he had hid for too long, but what choice was there?

He walked past the bar, sniffing the beer and the cigarettes, around the block, again into the edge of the neighborhood, a closed used car lot, the used music store and stood in front of the radio station.

He waited for a moment outside, reading the red and yellow posters on the front window announcing the school play and the circus coming to town.

Finally he ducked inside, yanking his pistol from his pants at the same instant that the smiling receptionist said good morning and raised both hands into the air.

He moved quickly around the corner, past offices, to the big window with ON THE AIR in red letters above the door.

Two laughing men sat inside the glassed studio around a big horseshoe desk with padded black chairs and hanging microphones, plaques and a clock on the wall.

They waved as he stood there watching.

The man tried one door, trotted around the corner to another and then approached a third entrance to the glass studio.

Behind him he heard a pounding on the carpet as the front desk woman and the men from the offices hurried after him.

Shoving the gun under both arms he hurtled into the last door.

And he was inside.

The laughing men now swiveled with curious looks toward him in their big chairs.

The man held up the gun as he moved to the one empty chair.

At the last moment he took a big step back to the door and flicked the lock closed, just as many hands fell on the handle.

The speakers in the corners of the outside hallway waited, silent. Dead air.

The people heard the police sirens in the street.

They heard the man telling the radio show hosts something they did not understand, and noticed that the laughing men looked nervous.

They stared at him, one with folded pink hands on the big desk, the other with his fingers tight on his padded chair arms.

The man sat.

He pointed the gun at the closest man.

"Show me how this works," the crowd in the hall heard him say.

The radio show host walked over on tiptoes, flicked a switch, adjusted the microphone height.

"I want this to be on the air," said the man as he waved the radio man back to his place with the long barrel of his gun.

The radio show hosts exchanged pensive looks with each other and the growing crowd in the hall, now including policemen with guns held high in two hands.

Police car lights bounced off the hair salon windows, the exercise place, the closed movie theatre, and the refrigerator store.

A crowd gathered below the outside speakers at the front door of the radio station, listening to the man who had taken over the morning radio show.

Hmmm.

People in cars, in offices, in the schools, the sale barn, in the fast food restaurants, stopped what they were doing and listened.

While he pointed the gun, back and forth, at the two men, he pulled from his pants a blue notebook.

He spread the notebook on the table as if an altar, smoothed it down flat as he could, picked a lettuce shred, and began to page through.

"Chapter one," he said, judging how far his mouth should be from the microphone.

"Can you hear this?"

He swiveled to address the people behind him, pointing at the speakers with his gun.

Heads nodded.

He swung back.

"Well, then ... Gob Bless America."

The man began, pausing to sweep away some few bits of white dust from the page, and just then remembering.

He partially stood and pulled from his front pocket a pair of black-rimmed glasses and put them on. He pulled tight his red cap and began anew.

"Dog Bless America."

He took a deep breath, pointing the barrel of the gun back and forth in the general direction of the men across the table like a lighthouse beam as they ducked each time it came close.

"And Doug Bless The America People and the New Night-ed States Of American."

About the author

Mike Palecek has worked on newspapers in Minnesota, Iowa, Nebraska and South Dakota. He also produced Penn Magazine, and was a co-founder of Moon Rock Books, along with Jim Fetzer, as well as co-hosting, along with Chuck Gregory, The New American Dream Radio Show. He has written several novels, information about those available here: https://mikepalecek.newdream.us

Now retired after working for twenty years with the disabled, Palecek also served five terms in jail and prison for protests against U.S. military policy, and was the Iowa Democratic Party 5th District candidate for the U.S. House of Representatives in the 2000 election, receiving 65,500 votes.

(Banned from Canada.)

(Palecek video presentations)
Freedom of the Press False Flags & Conspiracies Conference 2020
https://www.bitchute.com/video/PBDaf07tMm5K/

Freedom of the Press False Flags & Conspiracies Conference 2021
https://153news.net/watch_video.php?v=WGDSDUSWSM78

Archives for The New American Dream Radio Show
https://newdream.us

Allison Healy - Artist

Raised in the Northwoods of Minnesota, Allison developed a deep
connection to the natural world as well as a great attention to detail, a
theme that carries through much of her work. She left high school two
years early and received an associate degree in liberal arts, with a focus
in literature and fine art at the age of eighteen. Earning a Bachelor of
Fine Arts degree in illustration from the Minneapolis College of Art &
Design, she also spent some time abroad intensively studying illustration
and graphic design at the University of Brighton, on the south coast of
England. Her work has appeared on a range of publications, including but
not limited to: book covers, children's books, magazines, album covers,
greeting cards, and several applied graphics for various products.
She iscurrently living and working in Boston, Massachusetts, where her studio
is now based.

www.ingramcontent.com/pod-product-compliance
Lightning Source LLC
Chambersburg PA
CBHW020631130626
46552CB00003B/1170